RAYE MORGAN

Abby and the Playboy Prince

THE ROYALS OF
MONTENEVADA

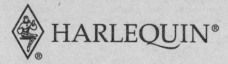

HARLEQUIN®

TORONTO • NEW YORK • LONDON
AMSTERDAM • PARIS • SYDNEY • HAMBURG
STOCKHOLM • ATHENS • TOKYO • MILAN • MADRID
PRAGUE • WARSAW • BUDAPEST • AUCKLAND

ISBN-13: 978-0-373-17536-9
ISBN-10:   0-373-17536-1

ABBY AND THE PLAYBOY PRINCE

First North American Publication 2008.

Printed in U.S.A.

THE ROYALS OF
MONTENEVADA

Three gorgeous princes...
and how they meet their brides-to-be!

The whole kingdom is in an uproar.
As the princes fulfil their duties, a rumor starts
that one special woman is carrying a royal heir.
A massive search reveals three single mothers...who might
be perfect for the three Montenevada sons. Could love be
part of the royal baby bargain?

Find out in August—October 2008 with this
exciting new miniseries by Raye Morgan:

Last month:
The Prince's Secret Bride:
Meet Nico, who never expected to encounter
a pregnant woman with amnesia...much less marry her!

This month:
Abby and the Playboy Prince:
Mychale discovers a tempting woman living in his house,
then finds out she's hiding a secret baby....

Next month:
Found: His Royal Baby:
Dane never forgot her, then he learned
they had a child together. Could they
finally become the family he's always wanted?

To E.M. for your limitless support.
You brighten the lives of all around you!

CHAPTER ONE

PRINCE MYCHALE of the royal house of Montenevada came fully awake, staring into the darkness. He'd been dreaming again. His body was tight as a fist. Even in sleep, he couldn't relax.

Groaning, he rolled out of bed and headed to the attached bathroom as thunder rumbled nearby. He reached automatically for the light switch, then swore softly when it didn't work and he remembered the electricity probably hadn't been on in this vacation chalet for months. As though in answer to his wishes, a flash of lightning lit the room and he saw himself in the mirror for two seconds.

He looked like hell. But what did he expect? He hadn't slept for days. He'd walked right off the yacht in Cannes where some film star whose name he couldn't remember had thrown him a party, jumped into his Lamborghini, peeled out of the marina parking lot and kept on going. He'd driven into the dawn, and then through the next day, crossing borders, ignoring speed limits, until he was home.

Home, the center of his support—the focus of his discontent. His home was in the tiny country of Carnethia, where he was third in line for the throne. Instead of heading for the palace, he'd turned his car toward this remote mountain retreat, which was empty now, but had been his family's refuge during the recent war. He needed time to clear his mind and decide what he was going to do. Time alone.

He turned on the water and was grateful to get a gush out of the faucet. At least that was still on. He would have to ignite the pilot on the water heater as soon as it was light. Then he could wash away Stephanie's smell. Her perfume lingered like a bad dream. Stripping off his shirt, he dropped it to the floor, then reached to cup his hands under the water and wash his face.

"Ouch."

He drew back quickly. The water was hot.

"What the hell?"

That wasn't right. No one would have closed up the house and left the pilot on. Strange.

But he was too tired to deal with that now. He adjusted the water, washed his face and slouched back to throw himself on the bed. Despite the thunderstorm approaching, he was instantly asleep.

Abby Donair crept silently to the door of the prince's bedroom and listened intently. She couldn't hear a thing. Was he still in there? She had to know. But more than that, she had to have the ring of keys he'd picked up in the butler's entry and taken into the bedroom with him. Without those keys, she couldn't get to the supplies, and there was something in the locked pantry that she needed badly.

What bad luck to have the prince show up like this. She'd known this château since she was a child and knew from experience how to get inside, even though the place had been empty since the restoration of the monarchy earlier that year. So when she was looking for somewhere to hide, the royal chalet had seemed a natural. She'd thought it would give her a sanctuary and a respite, a place to catch her breath and prepare for what she had to do next. And now this.

She closed her eyes for a moment, trying to think of any other way she could get into the pantry. She didn't want to open the bedroom door. She knew chances were good she wouldn't get away with what she was planning. But short of taking an ax to the pantry door, there really wasn't a viable alternative.

Thunder rolled, reminding her there was no escape. Not tonight. Probably not in the morning, either. Oh, why did he have to show up on this very night? After all her careful plotting, all the preparations she'd made. No one from the royal family had been here in months. She'd been so sure it would make the perfect safe haven for her. And then, out of the blue, Prince Mychale had shown up. Why now?

But moaning did no good. She had to act. Tucking back her long, straight blond hair, she held her breath and turned the knob on the solid oak door, peeking in.

There he was. She could make out his form lying crosswise on the wide bed. Lightning lit the room for a moment and she saw him better. Her heart began to pound. He looked half-naked. And maybe more. The way he was twisted in the sheets, she couldn't really tell.

But that didn't matter. Hopefully he wouldn't wake up. If he did, all bets were off and she was in big trouble.

In his eyes, she would just be some tramp who'd broken into his house. The man had been trained as a warrior, even though from what she'd heard, the war had ended before he'd had a chance to do much fighting. Who knew what he would do to her?

Another flash of lightning revealed the object of her quest. There on the nightstand she could see the master ring of château keys, right next to his wallet. Taking in a deep breath and gathering her light nightdress around her, she started toward them.

A floorboard creaked as her bare foot touched it. She winced and bit her lip, but she kept on moving. If she just kept going and grabbed the keys, she could be out of here in less than…

He moved, groaning softly. She went very still, holding her breath. Morning was coming and despite the storm, the room was growing lighter. Now that she was near, she could see him pretty well. She'd seen him often enough in the past and she'd always thought he was the best looking of the three royal brothers. But looking at him now, she thought he was more beautiful than ever, his skin sleek, his body hard and shaped to tempt caresses. She'd never been this close to him before. Were her fingers trembling? Oh Lord! For just a second, she was afraid she was losing her nerve.

But no. Failure was not an option. Gritting her teeth, she leaned over him, stretching for the keys. Just an inch more, just a second more…

Her fingertips had barely touched the metal when it all went wrong. He moved. She flinched. And suddenly he'd grabbed her and she was flat on her back, pinned to the mattress.

"Oh!" she cried, the breath knocked out of her for a moment.

"Looking for something?" he asked coldly, his face inches from hers.

She gasped. When she'd considered the dangers involved in what she was doing, she had never pictured the outcome quite this way. He was holding her down by her wrists and his long, hard body was on top of hers. She'd never been under a man's body before. How could it be so scary and so thrilling at the same time?

"Let me go!" she cried, struggling for only a moment. The more she tried to move beneath him, the worse things got.

"Can't do that," he said calmly. He was almost smiling now, as though the first shock of finding her leaning over his bed had passed and he was more amused than alarmed. "If I let you go, I'll have to wake up from this dream, and I rather like it so far."

She glared up at him. It was humiliating to realize he thought so little of her chances of doing anything to hurt him that he could take this so casually. And even joke about it! That made her furious. All her fears faded as she took in the indignity of it all.

"What is the matter with you?" she demanded. "Or do you always welcome strange women into your bed like this?"

"I don't know." His face came nearer and the next thing she knew he'd moved in closer and was nuzzling against the side of her neck, breathing in her scent as though he enjoyed it. "You don't actually seem all that strange to me," he murmured huskily.

She drew in a sharp breath and alarm shivered

through her. What was he doing? She'd heard stories about this prince, lurid tales of sexual escapades and romantic adventures whispered by women who seemed to know what they were talking about. Maybe he was used to making love to any woman who happened to tumble into his bed. Maybe he thought this sort of thing was normal.

Well, despite the fact that his face against her skin was deliciously seductive, *she* wasn't used to it and she didn't think it was normal. In fact, she wouldn't put up with it at all.

"Get away from me!" she cried, trying to twist to the side.

He drew back, looking down at her, but still holding her prisoner with his body.

"You know, I was just lying here, sleeping peacefully," he noted, "and *you* were the one who invaded *my* space."

He was right and she had to admit it. She was still glaring at him, but her heart wasn't pounding in her throat any longer. Maybe she could think things over a bit more rationally now. Maybe it was time to try another angle.

"I'm sorry," she said, trying to sound sincere and only partially succeeding. "I...I didn't mean to. I was just... Well, I wasn't trying to wake you. I thought I could just get in and out without bothering you."

He was studying her face as though this whole thing was puzzling him. Despite everything, she couldn't help but notice how appealing he looked with his dark hair falling over his forehead. There was nothing between them but her light cotton nightgown and a thin, silky sheet and she was beginning to feel more of him than was safe.

"I...I'll just go now," she added hopefully.

His brilliant eyes were heavy-lidded as he gazed down at her. "You promise?"

She blinked up at him. "Promise what?"

"That you'll go? Maybe go burglarize some other house and let me sleep?"

"Uh…"

He meant it. She realized his voice sounded groggy. He really was tired and he really did just want her to leave him alone. At least, that was the way his words came across to her. That was a relief. The trouble was, she couldn't do what he was asking. Not really.

Reading her mind by the look on her face, he groaned, closing his eyes for a second. "You don't want to go, do you?"

"I…well, it's raining." She was only pointing out the obvious.

"I see." He looked exhausted. "So you're not planning to go anywhere when you come right down to it."

She couldn't lie to the man—not about this anyway. "Well, no, not until the storm passes. You can't expect me to…"

He was laughing. Softly laughing, but laughing nonetheless. She frowned up at him, offended.

"What's so funny?"

"You." He rolled off her and lay back against the pillows. "You haven't been at this burglarizing business long, have you? Maybe you ought to rethink this as a career path. You don't seem to have much of a knack for it."

Pulling herself up to a sitting position and pulling her nightdress decorously around her knees, she glared down at him. "I wasn't trying to burglarize you."

He frowned as though all this was just too much to deal with right now. His gaze flickered over her, lingering on where her breasts were easily visible beneath the flimsy fabric.

"Well, if this was an attempted seduction, you need a few pointers in that realm as well." He yawned. "But I'm afraid I'm going to have to pass for now. I can barely keep my eyes open and..." Suddenly he frowned, staring at her in the morning gloom. "Wait a minute. Do I know you?"

"I..." She thought fast. It was probably safer to let him know they did have a connection of sorts. He was going to find out eventually anyway. "My name is Abby Donair. You've probably seen me before. Maybe here in lake country in the old days. Or more recently, at the palace. I've been living with my uncle, Dr. Zaire."

His brow cleared with recognition. "Ah yes, the good doctor. The man who knows all our deepest secrets."

"I don't know about that." She looked at him sharply, wondering what he meant and pretty sure it wasn't good. Quickly she tried to make things clear. "I mean, he's never told me anything about you."

"Good." He squinted at her. "Yes, I remember you now. You were just at my sister's birthday luncheon last month, weren't you? I think I remember noticing you. You played a piece on the piano."

She nodded reluctantly, remembering with embarrassment that she hadn't exactly stunned the world with her musical talent that day. "Yes, that was me bumbling my way through 'Moonlight Sonata'. I was horrible."

He grinned. "I guess I wasn't listening very well. I remember thinking you were cute as a button."

She gaped at him in astonishment, surprised that he would even have noticed her at all.

But he wasn't in the mood for conversation. He sighed heavily. "God, I'm just so tired. I'm treading water here. I've got to sleep. Can we continue this later?"

"Oh. You mean…?"

"I mean, I should be ushering you off the premises and generally acting like the property owner I'm supposed to be, but I can't seem to summon the energy. So I'm going to trust you not to slit my throat or rob me blind. Okay?"

"Okay." She gave him an exasperated look. "I don't really foresee getting the urge to do either, if you want to know the truth."

"Great. I'll just sleep on top of my wallet so as to remove all temptation." He reached out to take the wallet off the nightstand and put it under his pillow. Then he yawned again. "Okay. Then I'll see you in a few hours. Good night."

He closed his eyes, sank down into the pillows and seemed to drift off with no further ado. She stared at him. He really was the most gorgeous man she'd ever seen this close. The rounded muscles of his shoulders and upper arms made her bite her lip, and as she followed the hard planes of his chest down to where his flat stomach muscles tightened around his navel, then disappeared beneath the sheet, for a second or two, she forgot how to breathe. Greek statues had nothing on this man.

Very carefully, she regained her composure and then slipped off the bed and padded to the door. She looked back for a moment, then stepped into the hallway and closed the door behind her.

"Well, that wasn't as bad as it could have been," she murmured to herself hopefully. With a mischievous smile, she pulled the ring of keys out of the deep pocket of her nightdress. She'd done what she'd come to do anyway and now she had access once again to the pantry where she'd stored the baby formula.

"Just another couple of minutes, Bree-baby," she murmured softly, though she knew the little infant couldn't hear her at this distance. "I'll have your bottle for you. Just hold on." With a sigh of relief, she hurried toward the kitchen.

The rain turned to light drizzle a little before noon. Abby was pacing nervously through the casual breakfast area, wondering just how much longer the prince would sleep. She'd prepared a three-course breakfast with cinnamon rolls, fruit salad, a spiced frittata, sausages and rich, dark coffee. Luckily, the kitchen was well stocked with canned things, but she'd had to use a couple of the precious fresh eggs that she'd bought at the train station to round out the meal, and if he didn't come down soon, it would hardly be worth it. The table was set. Everything was ready. It was all part of her plan to win him over to her point of view.

She had the perfect scenario in mind. He would come down, fully rested, and she would have this nice breakfast prepared and laid out and he would smile and turn to her in surprise, then thank her.

And she would smile back as he sat down to eat and ask nicely, "Do you mind if I stay here for a couple of days? I just need a place where I can be away from everyone else and think about my life for a while."

And, full of good food and rested cheer, he would see that she meant him and his family no harm, that she was really good-hearted and he would say, "Sure, be my guest."

After all, he was probably headed to a party or a country weekend or a romantic tryst or whatever. He'd obviously just stopped here to sleep and would be on his way once he was rested. Would he let her stay here if she asked? She wasn't sure, but she didn't know what else to do. She couldn't run for the border in this weather, not carrying a baby. The fact that he knew her uncle well ought to help. After all, Dr. Zaire had been permanently attached to the royal family for generations. She didn't see any reason why things shouldn't go just the way she was planning.

In her mind she could see him finish his meal, sigh happily, then get up to leave, waving goodbye as he went, perhaps calling back, "Take good care of the old place for me, won't you?"

"Of course," she would respond as he got back into that fancy car she'd watched arrive with such anxiety the night before and drove off into the mist toward— whatever place he was on his way to.

Simple. Logical. Why not?

There were only a few things that could make it all go wrong. The first was the fact that the food she had prepared so carefully would get so cold it would turn to cement if he didn't come down to eat soon. And the second was…what if the baby cried?

Baby Brianna. She threw a glance at the stairway. There was no sign that the prince was awake. Quickly she made her way to the back of the house, to the tiny maid's room where she had the baby in a makeshift crib, fashioned from a dresser drawer and some baby blankets.

A wave of emotion hit her as she looked down at the sleeping child her sister had given birth to less than two months before. Protecting Bree was all she cared about now. She was such a pretty baby with her downy peach fuzz hair and her rounded pink cheeks.

"I'm going to be your mommy from now on, sweetheart," she whispered, tears welling in her eyes as she thought of her sister's tragic death. "I just hope I can do a decent job of it. I promised Julienne, and I'm going to try as hard as I can to keep that promise."

The promise was the last thing she'd said to her sister as she lay dying. She hadn't realized how soon she would have to put her promise to the test. As soon as she'd understood what her uncle was planning, she knew she had to get her sister's child out of his control. Luckily, he'd been so consumed with his plotting that he hadn't noticed the time she took to come here to the chalet and prepare to bring Brianna here.

This was to be the first step on their journey. The plan was clear. She would get on a bus, just like they'd taken to get here in the first place. As they neared the border, she would get off and head for the countryside. They might be intercepted, and just in case, she'd printed up some fake id cards on the computer. They ought to pass if no one looked too closely.

But she wasn't really worried about that part of the trip. She'd done it many times before with her family when she was young. During the recent war, it had sometimes been the only way to get from her grandparents' estate in Dharma back into Carnethia. She knew the route and how to avoid the checkpoints. It would be harder carrying the baby, but she could do it. She would be in Dharma in just a couple of hours, and from there it was just a short train ride to Northern Italy.

And then—what? Yes, that was the question.

Brianna's tiny baby lips puckered for a moment, but then she sighed, still asleep. Abby smiled through her tears. She couldn't keep thinking about the suffering in her life. For Brianna's sake, hope was going to be the watchword from now on. Hope for a beautiful future. Hope would make her strong.

That, and just a little luck ought to do it.

Mychale closed his eyes and enjoyed the water as it beat down on his long, lean naked body. The water pressure was great here, all that energy from the mountain rivers. A shower such as this was like a good massage. If only he could beat the kinks out of his mind the same way.

He'd had a fantasy the night before of washing away Stephanie's scent, as though that would somehow help clear up the Stephanie problem. But in the bright light of day, he knew that wasn't going to work. Stephanie was here to stay and he was stuck with her. The wedding was scheduled for the fall.

He groaned. The whole thing was insane. How had he let his brother Dane talk him into this? But he knew exactly how. All that guilt-inducing rhetoric about duty and honor and what he owed his country and the royal house of Montenevada. He'd let Dane wear him down and now he was betrothed to a woman he could barely stand to be in the same room with. Something had to give, and he was here to figure out what that something was.

He felt better after a shower, clean and fresh and almost fully rested. He was going to find a way out of his quagmire. No problem. He would think of something. For just a moment, a wave of nausea came over him and he leaned against the wall, wondering what the hell was going on. But it evaporated quickly, leaving him with a slight sense of unease, but not much more. He would probably feel better after he ate something. And that was contingent on there being any food in the house.

He pulled on slacks and a clean shirt out of the closet. As he was buttoning his cuffs, he remembered about Abby Donair and groaned again. Another problem woman to deal with. But maybe their encounter had scared her off. Most likely, once she realized she wasn't going to have the run of the place on her own, she'd headed out to greener pastures. The sound of rain against the windowpanes put a damper on that idea, but he kept his optimism alive.

He went down the stairs with a spring in his step. He'd always loved this big old house with its massive fireplaces and the dark wood and glass everywhere. In its day, it had seemed state-of-the-art for the sort of mansion that hung off the side of the mountain, but now it could certainly use a bit of updating. The plumbing was ancient and the colors were gloomy. He should make some plans and come up here to oversee the renovations. He could put in top-of-the-line modern appliances, granite counters in the kitchen, travertine tile in the bathrooms, maybe a sauna or two, an environmental rain room. Maybe he should move in for good, give up his playboy lifestyle and start living the life of a country gentleman. Why not?

He knew he wasn't serious, and it made him smile to think about it.

But his smile died as he came face-to-face with Abby in the hallway. She stared at him and he stared at her and neither of them said a word, as though both were judging what to make of the other after their unusual meeting earlier that morning.

He studied her, trying to place her in a category for more comfortable judgment. She was pretty, but very young, her body nicely rounded but slender. Her long blond hair hung straight as a silk banner down her back, reaching almost to her cute little derriere. She looked like a university coed, or a throwback to the Summer of Love. He could picture her dancing to psychedelic music, spinning with a dreamy look on her face and her hair flying behind her.

"So you weren't just a midnight fantasy after all," he said at last.

Her dark eyes flashed and suddenly she didn't look so young. "Of course not," she said, her voice ripe with disdain.

"Still, that leaves us with a question hanging in the air," he noted cynically. "What the hell are you doing here?"

CHAPTER TWO

ABBY stared into Prince Mychale's mocking gaze for a long moment without even trying to answer his question. Something told her that, if she wasn't careful, this could turn out very differently from her fantasy picture of a few moments ago. Drawing in a quick breath, she turned on her heel and began to walk down the hall.

"Come this way," she said crisply over her shoulder. "I made you some breakfast."

He had to grin at her high-handed manner. It was so obviously bravado, but why not? She needed to maintain a sense of herself and she'd come up against royalty. This was certainly better than the cringing tone some took around him. He had to admire her nerve.

So he followed, enjoying the way the length of her hair teased the rounded seat of her snug designer jeans, though he was a little too jaded to have his head turned by such simple pleasures. At least, that was what he was telling himself as he walked along with his gaze glued to the pertinent part of her anatomy.

She opened the door to the breakfast room. Floor-to-ceiling windows brought in a flood of light despite the rain. When he was young, this had been his favorite room in the house, the place where he'd read voraciously from the chalet library while the kitchen staff supplied him with drinks and snacks, along with the occasional lecture from Milly, the family cook, in the proper food etiquette for princes. She had a few helpful words for his choice of reading material a time or two as well. He remembered when she'd found a risqué magazine he'd hidden between the pages of his history book. The place had erupted like Vesuvius that day. Even his eyebrows had felt singed.

Memories flooded him for a moment, bringing on a certain melancholy. Where were all those servants now? They'd been like family back then, closer to him than his father and brothers who were off fighting while he was still in school. The house seemed an empty echo chamber without them.

But never mind. He had this lovely young woman instead, much as she tended to puzzle him, especially as he looked at the breakfast she'd prepared.

"Why?" he asked, his tone appropriately bemused.

She glanced back as she went into the kitchen to get the coffee urn. "You have to eat."

She was right. That still didn't explain why she should be the one to feed him, but she was right. He surveyed the room narrowly, but he was ravenous. He hadn't had anything for over twenty-four hours. And the things she'd laid out on the table looked great.

"You didn't put knockout drops in the coffee, did you?" he asked as he sat down at the table and watched her pour the dark liquid into his porcelain cup.

She grunted, flashing him a sideways glance. "You've already slept long enough."

As though she resented it! He looked up at her and shook his head. If she really was as young as he'd presumed, she didn't seem to know it. She was acting like a stern schoolteacher, or even dear old Milly.

He frowned, remembering how she'd felt in his bed just a few hours before. That lithe body writhing beneath him hadn't given a hint of her autocratic side. And just the thought of it made him want to study her rather delicious form more closely. He glanced in her direction, admiring the way her light sweater clung to the generous swell of her breasts. One look and he was reacting like a teenager. Clearing his throat, he carefully reined in his libido and regained control of his incorrigible imagination.

"Correct me if I'm wrong," he noted dryly, taking a sip of the hot coffee and wincing at the sting. "But I'm the homeowner, aren't I? And you're the housebreaker? Or do I have that switched somehow?"

"I haven't broken a thing," she countered indignantly. "And I'm being very nice to you. Don't forget about not biting the hand that feeds you."

"With ingredients from my own pantry, no doubt," he muttered as he savored a bite of the cinnamon roll. It was melt-in-your-mouth great, he had to admit. The woman could bake, at least. "Unless you brought along some supplies of your own?" He looked up in an ironic bit of challenge.

She had the grace to color slightly. "No, not really. Except for the eggs."

She'd brought along her own eggs. Somehow that didn't sound like your average housebreaker. More like a squatter, perhaps. That thought gave him a second of pause, but he dismissed it out of hand. She was no squatter. She was here for a reason. He had no doubt he would find out what that reason was, eventually.

"If you're not a housebreaker, how did you get in?" he asked curiously.

For the first time, a look of pure guilt flashed in her eyes. She hesitated and he could almost see the decision-making process as it took place and she tossed out the excuses that first came to her in order to tell the truth.

"When I was young, we would come up here when the Royal family left. We…well, we figured out how to get in."

He stared, appalled at the nerve. "You little thieves!"

"No! Oh, no, we never took anything." Her eyes radiated complete honesty and despite his usually cynical nature, he reluctantly bought it fairly quickly. Still, that was a danger signal and he knew it.

"We just…absorbed the atmosphere." She hugged herself, looking around the room, letting memories creep back. The war had seemed far away, but they were all aware of it looming off in the distance, like a dark cloud menacing the horizon. Larona, the village, was divided, just as the country was, but most there backed the royal family. After all, they had lived among them for generations. "We tried to imagine what it would be like to be princesses," she added softly.

"Who's 'we'?" he asked gruffly, breaking off another piece of roll and savoring it.

She looked surprised. "My sister and I." And a

very young Gregor Narna. But she didn't need to bring him into this. Memories of her sister were troubling enough.

Gregor had been the instigator of the break-ins. His father was the village veterinarian so he'd accompanied him here to the château many times to care for one or another of the horses that had been kept here in those days. Gregor himself was on a fast track to medical school, even then.

"Someday I'll have a house like this," he would tell his wide-eyed audience of two as they wandered through the rooms and spoke in whispers, just in case. "Just wait and see."

How Julienne had laughed at him. "It's not the house you care about," she'd teased him. "You just want another glimpse of Princess Carla. We all know it!"

Abby smiled, remembering how red-faced Gregor had been as he stoutly denied it. Dear Gregor. She hadn't seen him for years, but at that time, he'd been like a beloved older brother to her and Julienne. Then their parents had died and they'd left the Larona and the lake country to go live with their uncle, and things had never been the same.

Her eyes clouded as she thought of that and she turned away. "We never touched anything," she said again. "We were just little girls. Coming here was like coming to an enchanted world. We loved it."

Mychale sat back in his chair and frowned. "Wasn't there a guard?"

"Oh, yes. There was that old bearded man who liked to walk the grounds with a shotgun over his shoulder." She smiled remembering. "He spent most of his time fishing, though, in the river. He was easy to avoid."

"Elias Karn." He nodded, remembering the man. "I guess we'd better hire a replacement. You're lucky we've been ignoring the old place since the restoration."

"I know. I checked that out before…" She stopped dead. She'd almost said, "before bringing the baby here." She was going to have to be more careful. "Before coming," she amended quickly.

"Did you?" He gave her a quizzical look. He still couldn't quite figure her out. "But I guess if old Elias had still been here, it wouldn't have held you back much. If he weren't already deceased, I'd dock his pension for inattention to his duties."

Her smile faded. He meant his threat in jest, but it betrayed a cold streak she didn't like. "So you're that type, are you?" she noted, sticking her chin out. "Like to throw your weight around? I suppose you use your royalty to get into dance clubs ahead of the others and go to the front of the line at fast food restaurants."

Her assumptions were so outrageously off the mark, he had to laugh. "You're merciless, aren't you?"

A rebellious look flashed across her pretty face. "I'm not a child," she said, as though somehow he'd implied she was.

"No," he agreed, cutting into more of the wonderful breakfast she'd prepared. "But you considered this your childhood haunt. And now you're back."

"But I won't be here long," she added quickly.

"You got that right," he muttered, his mouth full of the most delicious frittata he'd ever tasted. "I'll drive you down to the village as soon as the rain lets up."

"Oh, I can't go to the village," she protested, looking alarmed.

He stared at her. "Why not?"

"They…they know me there." Suddenly this young woman who had been so forthright was avoiding his gaze. "None of my family is left, but my family home was right in the middle of town. I'd be recognized in no time, and I really don't want anyone to know I'm here."

He frowned, remembering what she'd said the night before about being related to Dr. Zaire. "Doesn't your uncle know where you've gone?" he asked.

She shook her head. "No one knows. Except you, of course." She looked at him intensely. "Swear you won't tell."

"I'm not swearing anything."

He studied her for a moment, not quite sure what to make of her. He'd had women hide in his room before. He'd found women in his bed, had one climb up to a balcony to get to him. At first he'd thought she might be one of that type.

But now he realized this wasn't that at all. Sitting there, gnawing on her lower lip, she had trouble in her eyes. No, she was definitely not trying to entice him in any way. A faint grin played at the corners of his mouth. He rather liked the novelty.

"Where is it that you're going?" she asked him earnestly.

"Going?" It seemed an odd question.

She threw a hand out. "Well, I imagine you're on your way somewhere."

"No." He shook his head. She didn't seem to want to accept that this was still his base, his home. It had been for years while his family engaged in the violent rebellion that had finally taken back their government almost a year before. The mountain lakes area had never really been in the hands of the Acredonnas, the dictatorial regime that had kept this country in its sway for almost fifty years. Mychale and his family had often used it as their refuge throughout their long exile. Of course, in those days the perimeter of the estate was bristling with guards and firepower while the royal family was here. Who knew little girls sneaked right onto the property and violated all security rules whenever the entourage decamped?

Once the rebels had been tossed out and the monarchy had reestablished itself, the base of operations had shifted to the palace in the capital, but that didn't mean this area wasn't still important to the family. It was just as much their home as the palace was. Tradition and affection would make sure it always remained so.

"This was my destination," he told her, flexing his shoulders and looking around the room. "I'm here."

"Oh." She couldn't keep the disappointment out of her voice. "You're going to stay here?"

"That's the plan." He finished his meal and sighed with contentment, then looked at her. "Why do I get the distinct impression that you want me to go?"

She hesitated. "It's not that, exactly. But…" She took a deep breath and charged ahead. "Well, I was going to ask you if I could stay here. Just for a few days."

Her dark eyes beseeched him and he had to admit, they were awfully appealing. But the question was ridiculous. The woman wasn't a complete stranger to him, but it was close. And anyway, he'd come here to accomplish something that wasn't going to be easy. He needed room and focus, not an audience.

He shook his head emphatically. "Sorry. I'm going to be using the place."

She looked skeptical. "The whole place? All by yourself?" Her face changed. "Oh, maybe you're having friends join you?"

He groaned. "Oh, I hope not."

"Then…"

He felt a twinge and squelched it quickly. No, he could not let himself go soft.

"Listen…what was your name again?"

"Abby. Abby Donair."

"Abby Donair." His brow furled as he thought about that for a moment. He could remember her pretty face but he couldn't place the name.

"Listen, Abby," he went on. "I drove all the way out here in order to be alone. I've got some heavy thinking to do, and I can't do that with you hanging around. I'm sorry, but you're going to have to go."

Mychale sat back as though that settled the matter. It was more than obvious that he was used to people falling in line once he handed down the word. She wanted to glare at him but she knew that wouldn't get her very far. Still, wasn't that just like a prince? Or any man, for that matter.

She had just licked her upper lip, preparing an answer, when a new thought occurred to her. She looked at him sharply. She'd been thinking about herself, but she ought to be wondering why he would be out here in the middle of nowhere, needing to think things over. She could only think of one thing. It had to be because of the scandal that had been rocking the palace two days before when she'd taken off with her sister's baby. No wonder he seemed a bit out of sorts.

The whole royal family was in an uproar, from what she'd heard. Her main problem was going to be to keep him from connecting the whole affair to her—and Brianna.

"I guess all your family is pretty upset about… things," she began tentatively.

"Things?" He looked at her blankly. "What things?"

Her eyes widened in surprise. He didn't know about the scandal? Where had he been hiding? Didn't he pay any attention to the tabloids?

"Where have you been over the last few days?" she asked him bluntly.

He shrugged and looked uncomfortable. If only he could blot out that last week of his life. "On a cruise. Mediterranean."

"I see." Oh my. She was in luck, wasn't she? "No communication with the outside world at all, huh?"

"No." He frowned at her. "Why? Did somebody bomb the palace?"

"Not exactly." But kinda-sorta.

The bomb wasn't physical, though. It came in newsprint. But if he didn't know anything about it, he would never make any sort of connection to her. She could probably rest easy on that score. At least for now.

He was frowning, thinking back over his last few days. "Come to think of it, I have been incommunicado for too long. I didn't even listen to news on the drive up here, just music." He raised one dark eyebrow and looked at her openly. "So let's have it. What went wrong?"

"Wrong?" She blinked at him, casually innocent. "I didn't say anything went wrong."

He frowned suspiciously. She had said exactly that and

now she was equivocating. He wasn't buying it. "Maybe I should call home," he said, looking around the room.

"No telephone service," she reminded him with a shaky smile. "Everything's disconnected."

He patted his pocket and frowned. "I left my mobile in the car."

Her smile was wider now and she spread out her arms expansively. "No mobile service way up here, anyway, " she reminded him.

"Oh. That's right." Rising from the table, he shoved his hands into the pockets of his slacks and began to pace restlessly. "I suppose I could find a radio and…" His voice faded and he looked at her and sighed. "I know. No electricity." He frowned. "I assume you're the one who lit the pilot and turned the gas on. So why didn't you start the generator?"

She shrugged. "I wouldn't dare try to do that." She hesitated, then added, "And besides, turning on the lights would have given a signal to anyone down the mountain that someone was in here. And I didn't want to do that."

He nodded, agreeing with that sentiment all the way. Giving her a crooked grin, he asked, "Got any carrier pigeons handy?"

She shook her head, but her smile quickly faded. This little exchange was bringing home to her just how isolated the two of them were. And this prince had quite a reputation. Maybe she shouldn't be so cavalier about wanting to spend time with him—or in the same house, at any rate.

As though he read her mind, he stopped in front of where she was sitting and reached out to take her chin with his hand, tilting her face up toward his.

"Tell me, Abby," he said, looking down into her dark eyes with a mesmerizing light in his own. "What is the latest from the outside world that I don't know about?"

"Why, nothing." She made her eyes wide and innocent. "I can't think of a thing."

He didn't believe her and he didn't draw back his hand. Instead his long fingers flared out and made a long, slow stroke of her cheek, making her gasp softly. Her skin sizzled beneath his touch and her heart was beating just a little too fast. What was he planning to do?

"How long have you been here, anyway?" he asked.

"I…uh, only about one day." Meaning two. But who was counting at this point? There was a prince holding her face. Her mind was losing its moorings. Her ears were full of a strange buzzing sound and if she wasn't careful, she was going to lose her way in the depths of his deep blue eyes.

But suddenly his bright gaze faltered. He seemed to grimace and then he backed away, shaking his head and looking a little green about the gills.

"What the hell?" he muttered, reaching out to brace himself against the wall.

She stared at him, shocked to see him losing a bit of the tight control he usually maintained, but then she realized he must not be feeling well.

"Sit down," she ordered, slipping off the chair and touching his arm. "I'll put on a kettle and make you some tea. That'll help."

He shook his head and seemed to shake off whatever it was that had come over him.

"No, don't bother, I'm okay," he said, looking around

as though not sure whether to trust himself for a moment, but she had already left for the kitchen stove and was filling the kettle from the faucet. A nice cup of tea had been her mother's remedy for whatever ailed you, and she realized with a twinge that she seemed to have inherited the habit.

Coming back into the breakfast room, she studied him curiously. He still didn't look quite right but he wouldn't sit down. Instead he was standing at the tall window, looking out at the rain, which was now coming down in sheets again.

"If this keeps up, we're going to have to find Noah to build us an ark," he said.

"Noah mainly saves animals," she noted. "Two by two. Remember?"

He nodded. "So you're saying we're just flat out of luck?"

"Luck has nothing to do with it," she said stoutly. "We'll have to rely on our own resources."

Swinging around, he gave her a baleful look. "Tell me the truth, Abby," he said softly, his crystal-blue gaze traveling over her in a restless way. "If you were being forced into a situation where you were going to have to do something you absolutely hated, something that made you ill to think of, and yet you were told it was your sworn duty to do it, what would you do?"

She stared at him and her heart leaped into her throat. That was her own situation in a nutshell. How could he possibly know? "I…" She swallowed hard, trying to calm her pulse rate. "Your royal highness, I…"

He grimaced, then gave her a half grin. "Come come, Abby. It's just the two of us here, and we've already been to bed together. We won't stand on ceremony. Call me Mychale."

She shook her head, then resisted the urge to curtsy. "As you wish, your highness," she muttered, completely confused. What he'd just said led her to believe that he must know why she was here, why she was running from her uncle and his plans for her future. And if he knew, why wasn't he threatening her with prosecution? That was what any normal prince would do.

But no. Catching the look on his face and remembering how she'd probed for what he knew about the scandal and he'd been completely clueless, she realized she was jumping to a wrong conclusion. He was talking about something else, something that had him uneasy in his own right.

She took a deep breath and relaxed. Strange, but the few things he'd just said, including inviting her to refer to him informally, had reminded her of her place as nothing else had up to now. She was nervous as a cat, her fingers working at the hem of her sweater, wondering what he would say next.

But before he could say anything else, a sound wafted its way down the hallways and into the breakfast room where they were standing. The prince turned, frowning. "What was that?"

"The storm," she said quickly, turning back toward the kitchen. "You know how the wind can wail around an old house like this." She glanced back, ready to escape. "The water for your tea should be done soon. I'll just…"

"It's not the storm. There. Do you hear it?" He looked toward the back of the house. "What was that?"

"What?" She turned and listened, heart sinking. The

sound was unique and unmistakable. Brianna was calling out for a little adult attention.

"That noise. What is it?" He looked at her accusingly.

She swallowed hard and wished the thunder would come back. Brianna's cry was gathering steam.

"Uh, I don't know. The storm is probably..."

He turned on her, a look of astonishment in his deep blue eyes. "Abby, there's a baby in this house."

She shook her head, looking longingly toward the kitchen. "I think it's probably...uh, doves in the eaves," she tried.

His gaze crackled. "I don't think so." His look of pure skepticism stung. He just flat didn't believe a word she was saying. And why should he?

"It's a baby," he said evenly. "I know a baby when I hear one. Unless we've got gypsies in the closets, it's got to be yours." He shook his head, looking up as though appealing to heaven. "A baby. What next?"

She went scarlet. She might have known she would end up revealing the baby. Never mind. Her thoughts went into fever mode. Before he had a chance to turn her in, she would grab Brianna and be over the border, even if she had to do it in the rain. That was the answer. She would go back into her original plan of action. No problem. She'd been speculating all along that as soon as the weather cleared and things dried out enough, she would bundle the baby up and they would head for the neighboring country. That had always been in the cards. She would just have to shift things up a bit. Once she was over the border...

And once again, this was where the plan got a little rough. Where the heck was she ultimately going to go?

Somehow she'd been sure a good scheme would present itself once she got this far. Unfortunately that hadn't happened yet.

"Where'd the baby come from?" he was saying. He stood right in front of her, his face only inches from hers, his gaze demanding an answer.

She shrugged helplessly, head full of fears, heart full of tears. If he only knew how much that question hurt. "I…I can't…"

His gaze was cold now, cold and rather scary. "Come clean, Abby. Let's have it. The truth this time."

She was losing hope and she knew he could see it in her eyes. She would have to tell him something. She would give him some truth. But not the whole truth. She couldn't do that.

"Okay," she said at last, twisting her hands together. "I do have a baby with me." There. She'd said it. She closed her eyes for a moment, as though the world were about to fall on her.

But nothing happened. The prince didn't even speak. He just waited, watching her. She blinked, then hurriedly tried to fill the awkward silence with some sort of explanation. "So you see, that's why I couldn't leave. I couldn't take a baby out in this weather. I have to wait until the rain clears out. Surely you can see that."

He stared at her.

"I just need a place to stay until the rain stops," she tried again, but he wasn't listening.

"Let's go." He jerked his head in the direction of the tiny cries. "I want to see this baby."

She hadn't expected that. She blanched. She really didn't think this was a good idea. "Oh, but…"

"I want to see the baby. Now."

His gaze was cool and direct and his tone was downright royal. She suddenly sensed the power of his heritage. It swept over her like a physical force. She felt as though it had blown her hair back and she had to gulp to keep from losing her breath.

She wanted to argue. It was in her nature to protest when she thought something was not quite right. She tried. She felt the urge rise in her. But somehow she couldn't get the words out. And he began to look very large. Surely she wasn't scared of him—was she? Well, maybe, just a little bit. But she would never let him know.

Turning, she gave him a quick sideways glance and started toward the maid's room.

He followed right behind her.

CHAPTER THREE

ABBY PICKED up the baby and cuddled her against her shoulder, turning to look defiantly at the prince.

"Her name is Brianna," she said, her eyes daring him to say anything negative about the child. "She's two months old."

Prince Mychale made no attempt to come into the room. He stood in the doorway, his handsome face a picture of puzzlement, as though the underpinnings of his world had just given way and he was floating in a world he wasn't ready for.

"Why would you bring a baby to a place like this?" he asked as though he really couldn't understand it.

She blinked at him. "What's wrong with bringing a baby here? You were probably here as a baby."

"Right. With a full cadre of servants and nannies. With electricity and all the other accoutrements of modern life." He shook his head, looking disgruntled as he stared at her. "You bring a baby here in the middle of a huge storm. I don't even know how you got here. There's no car outside, except for mine." He frowned, shrugged and said, like a man at the end of his rope, "Abby, what the hell are you doing here?"

Any hopes that a baby would charm him flew right out the window. Abby bit her lip. How was she going to explain what she was doing here without letting on what she was really doing here?

Brianna had quieted, but only for a moment. Now she gave a shuddering sob and began to fuss a little. Abby pulled her out to where the prince could see her pretty little face.

"Don't worry, sweetheart," she cooed to the child. "He's just a big, bad old prince. I know he's scary looking, but he won't hurt you." She glanced at him from under her brows. "Try smiling," she advised. "That might help."

Smiling. Right.

He didn't feel like smiling. He was, in fact, beginning to feel more trapped than happy. He'd come out here to his childhood refuge to find some peace and quiet in order to think through a very important step he was about to take. And all he'd had since he got here was one distracting jolt after another. Including the shrill wail of the kettle now boiling away noisily in the distant kitchen.

Okay, this was just too much. He could hardly think straight, much less deeply. And now he was supposed to smile at the baby? No chance.

She kissed the baby's little round cheek. "You don't know much about babies, do you?" she said.

Babies? Since when did princes know anything about babies? It wasn't in his job description. "Sorry, we didn't cover child care in my classes at university," he said with just a hint of sarcasm.

"That's obvious," she said, and her flashing glance his way told him without words to watch his tone. She smirked at him. "They know when people hate them."

He shook his head in disbelief. How could she say such a thing? "I don't hate children," he protested.

"Really?" She looked intently into Brianna's face. "I don't know. She doesn't seem to think you like her."

"That's not true." What was not to like? She was a baby. Who didn't like babies? As long as they stayed in their own little rooms and in their own little play-yards where they belonged and didn't get in the way of adults. "I like her just fine."

"Really?" She looked up and held his gaze with her own, looking solidly accusatory.

He took a step into the room in his determination to prove it to her. "Abby, I like babies. Babies make the world go 'round. Every baby is a link in God's great daisy chain."

Oops. He probably hadn't done himself any favors with that last quip. The way her beautiful eyes were flashing, he could tell she didn't think it was especially amusing. Still, that didn't stop her.

She did have a moment of hesitation, remembering he wasn't feeling well. But he looked OK now. "Good," she said, moving fast. "Then you can hold her while I go fix your tea."

"What?"

By the time he realized what was happening and tried to back away, it was too late. He had a baby in his arms. And he was all alone. Abby was off toward the kitchen, calling back over her shoulder, "Take care to protect her head. Don't let it bobble."

"Bobble?" He repeated the word because he didn't know what else to do. "Bobble?" Here he was holding this sodden mass of baby flesh, fuzzy things draped all around it, staring down at two midnight-blue eyes that stared up at him as though he'd just landed on the nearest alien launch pad and might be contemplating a quick meal. If babies could fly, this one would be on its way.

"Uh, hi," he said hopefully. Hadn't Abby said to smile? He tried it and actually seemed to have a little success. "How are you feeling?" he asked.

The lower lip was trembling and the round eyes were filling with tears. A flash of pure panic rocketed through his soul. Smiles weren't working. Maybe a song.

"'That's why the lady is a tramp,'" he crooned.

The little girl drew in a shuddering breath and her shoulders began to shake.

"No, no, don't cry," he begged. "Look, funny faces." He tried one, then another. Things were only getting worse. Her eyes squeezed shut and her mouth twisted in agony as she let out an earth-shattering wail.

"No, no, no," he muttered, drawing her close in against his shoulder the way he'd seen Abby do it. "It's all right. Really it is. No one is going to hurt you." He gave the tiny back a few awkward pats and began to walk around the room. He cast a longing glance at the dresser drawer made up like a bed, but he didn't dare put her down there without consulting Abby first. He didn't have a doubt in the world that he would surely do something wrong if he tried it.

She was crying softly now, a baby in despair. He would have thought it would annoy him, but for some reason, it broke his heart instead. Poor little thing. She wanted her mom. Suddenly, out of nowhere, he found himself singing a song.

"Rock-a-bye baby, on the treetop."

Funny. He didn't even remember that he knew that song. It must have bubbled up from his subconscious. Either that, or it was in the ether, part of the zeitgeist, or whatever. He went on and on. He knew every damn word! And he found himself rocking back and forth to the rhythm the song created. What was going on here? Was he channeling another life? Or another level of his own existence? Maybe the experiences he'd had as a baby were stuck in his brain somewhere, just waiting to pop out at the right moment. In any case, it seemed to do the trick. The squirming little mass in his arms began to relax. The crying began to fade. He walked faster and sang harder.

"I think you've put her to sleep."

He looked up in surprise to find Abby back, smiling in the doorway. "I have?" It was true there was no more crying. And the little bundle he carried had gone from creating a painful burden to feeling like something rather wonderful. Funny.

Abby nodded, finger to her lips. "Here," she whispered. "Let me have her. I'll put her down." She took the baby from him and nodded toward the front of the house. "I put your tea on the table. Why don't you go on out? I'll join you in a minute."

He left gratefully. There was a certain amount of triumph in having put the baby to sleep, but that was all the celebration he needed right now. He'd prefer keeping out of the baby-sitting business. It was a comfort just to know that Abby and her baby wouldn't be here much longer.

Back in the living area, he returned to the window and stood staring out, feeling moody and a bit strange. He probably hadn't caught up on his sleep yet. Maybe that was why he felt like he couldn't quite get his balance at times.

But sleep wasn't what he'd come here for. Thinking. Planning. Finding a way to break his engagement to Stephanie Hollenbeck without getting disowned by his family and expelled by his country. That was the puzzle he'd come here to unravel. And he knew damn well he would need some peace and quiet to do it in. He'd come all the way out here to think about what he was going to do about Stephanie, and instead, he'd spent every waking moment so far dealing with a runaway girl and her baby. This was no good. No good at all.

"You see how perfect she is?" Abby said a few minutes later as she came into the room where he was still watching the rain and drinking his tea. "She really won't bother you. You will let us stay here, won't you?"

He looked down into her warm, dark eyes and winced, as though guarding against looking into too bright a light. She was much too appealing. Desire stirred in him in a way it hadn't in a long time. He'd begun to think he'd had so many women, he was growing immune to their charms. But looking at Abby, he had good, solid evidence that the old man-woman thing was still working for him. She was so close, her scent was teasing his senses just the way the sight of her small, shell-like ear was teasing his libido. He could imagine his tongue exploring that little ear. He could imagine his hands exploring that lovely body. He wanted her, and he hadn't denied himself much over the years.

Still, he knew he wasn't going to act on this urge. This was different from the usual. He couldn't just grab her and kiss her. She wasn't like the women who made careers out of being available for the men of his crowd. She wasn't at all like that. In fact, he knew instinctively Abby was the sort of woman who should be protected from that sort of life. But hey—someone should probably protect her from *him*. Since no one was stepping up to take over that little job, it looked like he was going to have to do it himself.

The thought put a crooked grin on his face, but he wiped it away before she saw it. He didn't want to give her the idea that she might talk him into anything. Because that wasn't going to happen. And not just because he didn't want company. There was too much he didn't know about her to let him feel comfortable. He still wasn't sure why she was here.

"So, what do you want for dinner?" she said brightly. "I'll fix us something that—"

"Abby," he broke in, trying to be stern, "you won't be here for dinner. I'm taking you and your baby down to the village as soon as possible."

She looked stricken. "I can't go down there."

"You once lived there. Isn't there someone who can take you in?"

Mutely she shook her head.

He was beginning to feel like an ogre. But what could he do? Abby scampering around in the background of his life just wasn't going to work.

"All right then, I'll take you to the train station."

Tears were welling in her eyes. He turned away, staring out at the rivers of mud running past the house and down the hill. He was a sucker for tears. He had to stay tough. Tough love. That was what he needed.

"Abby, what are you running from?" he asked simply.

She gave a little start of surprise before she answered. "My uncle."

"Dr. Zaire?"

She nodded and tried to smile. "I'm just like you. I needed some time alone to think things over. My uncle has made some plans for my life that I'm not sure I can accept."

"You, too?" He looked out at the rain, wondering if she'd made it up to give them a point of connection after he'd told her the bare outlines of his own problem. He frowned, wondering why his first response was always drenched in suspicion. When had he become such a cynic?

But it was a question hardly worth asking. He knew very well that he'd developed a thick skin in order to protect himself. He'd been lied to so often, that was all he expected from people. Everyone he came in contact with seemed to want something from him. Especially women.

"No husband?" he said, looking at her sideways.

"Who, me?" Then she realized what she was saying. "Oh. Uh, no, no husband."

"Ah, so that's the problem."

"No it's not." She shook her head stoutly. "I wouldn't want a husband. Having a baby is going to be trouble enough."

That seemed an odd way of putting it and he puzzled it over for a moment before he went on.

"My point was that I suppose your uncle isn't happy having an unwed niece with a child on his hands." His eyes actually showed real sympathy as his gaze met hers. "Abby, did he kick you out?"

Abby stared back at him for a long moment, then turned away, closing her eyes. How could she explain it all to him? It was a complete muddle in her own mind as it was. How could she tell him about her sister, Julienne, dying in childbirth in that wretched garret where she had her baby with a midwife instead of her uncle in attendance? How could she describe the doctor's anger when he found out what had happened, how it had fed into the resentment against the royal family he seemed to be blaming more and more? What would he think if she were to tell him that her uncle was plotting to pass Brianna off as Crown Prince Dane's missing child? Would he understand why she had to grab her sister's baby and make a run for it?

Probably—if she could only explain it all to him. But she couldn't. She didn't dare. And so, he would never really know.

"You're a strange girl, Abby," he said.

"No doubt." Turning back, she gave him a flippant smile meant to give cover to all her agonizing. "Not what you're used to, aye?"

"You got that right." There was a touch of irony in his tone and in the twist his mouth took on.

"But that's just it," she went on insistently. "I'm not at all the sort of woman you're accustomed to. I don't want any attention from you. I just want a place to stay, somewhere Brianna will be safe, for just a few days while we decide where we'll go next. You don't even have to acknowledge my existence if you don't want to. Just let me stay."

He put his arm up against the glass and leaned on it. He was feeling worse again, and that was making it harder to disappoint her, especially when he could hear that thread of candid emotion in her voice. If she started crying, he was going to have to leave the room.

"I'll stay out of your way, I swear. You won't even know I'm here."

He shook his head. "That's where you're wrong. It would be much easier not to know you're here when it's actually the fact." He grimaced, knowing he'd made a mess of that sentence but not caring enough to fix it at this point. He turned toward her. It was awfully hard to turn down such a sweet face. But he had to do it.

"Listen, Abby, I can't relax with a stranger slipping around in the shadows, trying not to bother me. It just won't work." He shrugged. "I'm sorry, but I'm going to have to take you down to the village."

She bit her lip and looked away. Tears were stinging in her eyes but she was bound and determined he wouldn't see them. She couldn't go to the village and she didn't dare take a train anywhere. Surely her uncle had agents in all the train stations by now. It would probably be safer to stay away from buses as well, but she couldn't walk all the way to the border, so she would have to risk it.

Looking out at the miserable weather, she shivered. She wasn't looking forward to this. But she had better hurry. She was going to have to wrap Brianna really well and take off before the prince knew they were leaving. She didn't want him to know which way she'd gone, either. Hopefully once he realized they were gone, he would shrug and forget all about them. That was the best outcome she could hope for now.

She glanced at him, realizing she might never see him again. Too bad. She was almost starting to like him.

"All right, then," she said, her voice just barely shaking. "I'll go get Brianna ready to leave. Give me an hour or so, okay?"

Turning, she left the room. He watched her go, pushing back the surge of regret it cost him. He almost called her back. He wanted to. But he felt so lousy.... She disappeared through the doorway just as a wave of nausea hit him, hard. It was like nothing he'd ever felt before.

"Oh," he groaned, reaching out to steady himself against the wall. He had to get somewhere safe. The room was spinning. Everything inside him was churning. He couldn't tell which way was up and which way was down, until he fell to the floor, and then he closed his eyes, moaning, and everything went dark.

CHAPTER FOUR

PRINCE MYCHALE was absolutely right, Abby had to go. What had she been thinking? Now that he was here, others would follow. The princes of the realm did not usually travel around alone. He had a pack of hangers-on somewhere, hunting for him no doubt. Maybe even some secret service officers who were supposed to be keeping track of him. At some point, the vultures would descend. His friends and brothers and the women who hung around him like rock star groupies would begin showing up soon. She'd watched this royal family from the sidelines long enough to know that. She had to get out of here.

In a strange way it was almost a relief. Now that she knew she had to go, her path was clear. There was no more room for doubts and questions about what she could possibly do to talk the prince into letting her stay. There was only one course before her and that included packing up Brianna and a few of her things as best she could and heading out into the rainstorm.

She set her jaw and felt fierce and determined, like a lioness forced to move her cub out of a danger zone.

She was going to have to get over the border by night-fall. Hopefully there would be a bus she could catch. If there wasn't, she would walk. She had to move quickly to get out of the house before the prince came looking for her. He would want to drive her down to the village and she couldn't do that.

Ten minutes later, she was stepping carefully around piles of slippery, soggy leaves, Brianna wrapped up like a sausage and held in a baby sling inside her coat—against her heart, she thought ruefully. Right where she belonged.

She glanced back at the house. It appeared cold and dark and empty-looking. She scanned the windows but didn't see the prince watching her go. That was lucky, of course, so why did she have a pang of disappointment that he wasn't waving her goodbye?

"Because you're acting like a big baby," she muttered as she turned back into the stinging wind. "Bree's more of a trooper than you are."

As she reached the end of the long driveway, she paused, looking back one more time. There wasn't a sign of life. With a sigh, she shifted the heavy backpack filled with diapers and formula to get a better grip on it. She had a hard trip ahead of her. But they would make it. They had to.

She turned onto the unpaved road that she knew would take her down to the far side of the mountain, where she should be able to hail the bus that used to go by every few hours. She remembered where her family used to get off, at a little rural grocery just inside the country line. They would stop in, buy a few snacks, then tramp into the woods, making for the border, and then on to the city of Dharma in the neighboring county.

Everyone knew where they were going and no one ever said a thing. Hopefully traditions hadn't changed.

"Ouch!"

She'd tripped on a rock and almost turned her ankle. Clutching Bree tightly with one arm, she reached out to steady herself against the rough wood fence with the other. She had to be more careful. If she let herself get hurt...

But even that fear faded as she realized what that jingling sound was—the sound she'd heard as she stumbled. She had the ring of master keys to the chalet still in her pocket. She'd forgotten to put them back. Her heart sank and she stood where she was, eyes closed.

What now? Could she just walk off and leave the prince stranded without the keys? There were many areas of the house he wouldn't be able to access without them.

"You've got to," a voice whispered insistently in her ear. "You have no choice. Drop them right here. He'll probably find them. Come on. There's no time to hesitate. You've got to get going."

Her hand slipped into her pocket and fingered the keys. She pulled the ring out and looked at it.

"Drop them right here!" the voice said again. "What else can you do?"

Bree sighed in her sleep. Abby's fingers tightened on the keys.

"Oh damn!" she cried, frustrated with herself, frustrated with luck. Or lack of it. She knew she wasn't going to drop the keys in the mud and hope he found them. She was going back. She had to.

The climb back up the hill was agonizing. Her wet hair was flopping over her eyes and Bree was beginning to squirm. By the time she made it to the back door of the kitchen, she was gasping for breath and feeling spent. Bree was making the noises that signaled a diminishing state of baby patience. This was no way to sneak into a royal château. But she wasn't going to leave the keys on the back porch after all this. Testing one key after another, she found the right one and slipped into the house. She was going to leave the keys right where they belonged, in the butler's pantry.

The house was so still. She placed the key ring on the marble tabletop and stood still, listening. There wasn't a sound. She bit her lip. Maybe she ought to take a peek in and see....

She was rather proud later, when she thought over what happened next, that she didn't scream. She didn't throw everything she was carrying up in the air, and she didn't faint. When she caught sight of the prince's body on the floor, she went very still. Freeze frame. Her heart stopped and everything went cold and mechanical inside her. Very carefully, she put down the backpack filled with diapers and bottles and then even more carefully, detached the sling and put Bree down onto the couch, safe into the back edge where she couldn't possibly roll off. There was a loud buzzing in her head, but she ignored it. Quickly she went to the prince and dropped onto her knees beside him.

He was breathing. Thank God. But his skin had a bluish tinge and he didn't look right at all. She touched him.

"Mychale?" she said, her voice quivering with fear. "Your highness?"

There was no response. And now there was something inside her that wanted very badly to scream, scream loud and long and let her close her eyes and wait for someone to come and tell her what to do. But no one was coming. It was up to her. There was no time for screaming.

The prince needed taking care of. Something was very wrong with him. She had no idea what it might be, but she knew she couldn't leave him this way. At the same time, she was terrified of moving him. What if that only made him worse?

She stared at him, adrenaline rushing through her veins. She could hardly breathe. What was she going to do? She glanced back at the remains of breakfast still left on the table. What if this was because of something she'd fed him?

What if…what if he died? A part of her knew what that would mean. She could see the headlines now. Not only had she allegedly stolen the crown prince's baby, but she'd killed his brother.

Never mind. First things first. She had to get a doctor. But how could she do that? She was on the run. She couldn't let anyone know. She looked down at Mychale's lean, handsome face and her heart flipped in her chest. There was no time to lose. She had to get him medical help. And she could do that if she could find Gregor Narna, her childhood friend who, the last she'd heard, was blazing a trail of honors in medical school. Would he be down in the house in the village where he had lived when she knew him? Why should he be there? It had been years since she'd seen him. He'd been away at medical school. Why would he come back here? She had no idea. But she didn't have any other options, did she? She would have to go down to the village and look for Gregor.

That meant she would have to take the prince's car. She

swallowed hard. She didn't have a driver's license. She'd tried driving a time or two. She and her sister had taken their uncle's car out for a crazy spin once when the doctor was out of town. But this time she would be driving a high-performance, very expensive car in the rain. The very thought terrified her. And even if by some weird chance she survived the drive, what if someone saw her?

But that wouldn't matter much in the end, because she would have crashed the car and killed herself by then. All very fitting if she were writing Shakespearean tragedies. But she was just hoping to get to someplace where she could live a normal life. Was that really too much to ask?

She steadied herself and cut back on the dramatics. She had to do this, regardless. The man's very existence was at stake. She grabbed a blanket to put over him, found his car keys, then picked up the baby and ran for the door.

Prince Mychale opened his eyes but he had to shut them again quickly. The room was still spinning around him, making him feel sick and helpless. His head was pounding like someone had taken a sledgehammer to it. What the hell was wrong with him? He couldn't move without wave after wave of nausea making him want to die. He lay as still as he could, trying to avoid total agony.

He couldn't think. Thinking only brought on more misery. He couldn't speak, couldn't move. The only thing he had besides enduring this torture was a blurry, fuzzy picture of a young woman. He knew, vaguely, that he'd just been talking with her, but he couldn't use his brain enough to name her. Whatever. It was enough, for now, to let her face swim in and out of his ragged consciousness. For now, she was all he clung to.

He could hear someone talking, but he couldn't open his eyes and see who it was. Someone was touching him. He frowned, trying to pull away, but the nausea left him utterly helpless. Something pricked in his arm, something stung, but the nausea was so much worse, he hardly noticed. He tried to open his eyes. Bare slits revealed her face floating above him. Relief trickled into the misery. He whispered a word and she bent closer.

"What?" she asked, leaning down to get as close as she could. "What did you say?"

He tried, but nothing was working the way it should. Closing his eyes, he gave it all he could conjure from deep inside. "Stay," he managed to get out at last, and then his world went black again.

"It's like a virus that attacks the inner ear," Gregor was saying, putting the syringe away in his black bag. He looked at Abby and shrugged. "I'm making a wild-ass assumption here, but the royal family has been prone to this sort of thing in the past. The symptoms are similar to Ménière's disease, but present in a much more extreme state. I've given him a dose of an antivertigo medication. Hopefully, if this is what I think it is, he'll begin to pull out of the worst of it very soon."

Abby nodded, staring at where the prince still lay on the floor. She'd put a pillow from the couch under his head and pulled the blanket up to his chin. She only hoped Gregor was right. The sight of Mychale like this, so vulnerable, so powerless, like a wounded tiger, twisted her heart.

She looked up at Gregor, grateful. He still looked very much like that bright, open boy she'd known so well, though he'd grown into a tall, handsome man. And there were obvious changes, such as the black patch he wore over his left eye.

"Thank goodness you were still in the same house, in the same room," she said, trying hard to keep her emotions in check. "I didn't know what I would find there."

He grinned at her. "Little Abby," he said softly. "It must be ten years since I last saw you and Julienne. How is she?"

Abby winced. "My sister died recently," she said woodenly, then shook her head as he began to respond. "No. I can't talk about it. Not now." She took a deep breath and tried to smile. "So tell me. What happened to you?" She gestured toward his eye.

His head went back. "The same thing that happened to all of us," he said a bit stiffly. "The war."

She gasped. "Oh, I'm so sorry. But I thought you were in medical school."

"I was." He shook his head. "I was in line for an internship in orthopedic surgery. But I couldn't let the restoration of the monarchy go on without me. I had to join during those last few months."

She nodded. His family had always been strong backers of the royal family. That was why she felt she could trust him with this visit to the château. With others, she would be afraid they might run straight to the tabloids. Gregor would never do such a thing. She had been so lucky to find him at home. If he hadn't been there, she didn't know what she would have done.

"And now?" she asked him.

"Well, surgery is out of the question, now that I've lost the use of my left eye."

"Oh, Gregor!"

"So I came home to reevaluate my options. Such as they are."

His tone was one of weary resignation, but there was a thread of bitterness there. How could there not be? She looked at him with complete sympathy but wasn't sure how to express it.

The prince stirred.

"Here he comes," Gregor said, looking relieved. "Good. We'll move him to the couch as soon as he can stand it. Then you'll have to help him for a day or so."

A day or so! Her mouth went dry. She couldn't do that. No. Maybe one more night. But by morning, she had to go. Brianna had to be her first concern. Which brought up another danger.

"Tell me," she said tentatively. "Is this thing he has…is it contagious? Is it something people can catch from him?"

He shook his head, amused. "No, Abby. You don't have to worry. You couldn't catch it if you wanted to."

That answer wasn't quite good enough.

"But, would others, say very young babies, be at risk?" she asked, fear slithering through her system. He didn't know about Brianna. She'd managed to keep the baby hidden in the back car seat when she was at his house and he had driven up here in his own car, arriving just after she'd stowed Bree back in the maid's room. Please don't let him get suspicious, she begged.

"Not at all," he told her. "But I don't expect any young babies to show up, do you?" He was looking at her more sharply. "You're not pregnant, are you?"

"No," she said quickly. "Would that make a difference?"

He shook his head again, but he was definitely beginning to wonder what all these questions were about. "You still haven't explained how you came to be here with him," he said.

He was being blunt, an old friend rather than a new doctor. She knew how this looked and she knew she was flushing as he stared at her. But she held her head high, determined he wouldn't get the idea that she felt guilty about anything.

"It's a long story," she told him. "I promise I will fill you in at some point. But right now, I'd rather not." She glanced pointedly at the prince and Gregor nodded, his attention back on his patient.

"How are you feeling?" he asked Mychale as his eyes fluttered open.

"Bad," the prince muttered, holding his head very still and only moving his eyes. "Very, very bad."

"Count to five for me," Gregor said, holding up his hand, five fingers spread in front of Mychale's face.

He did as asked, though very slowly and painfully. But Gregor looked pleased that he got the numbers in the proper order. "Good. We're going to move you to the couch."

"Oh, no, you're not," the prince stated flatly, his voice like whispered thunder.

Gregor grinned. "Don't worry. We'll give it a couple of minutes. We'll wait until you don't feel quite so rocky. And we'll help."

Mychale narrowed his eyes, looking up at him. "I know you," he said groggily. "You used to come up here with your father. He was our vet, wasn't he?"

Gregor nodded and gave a little bow. "Yes, your

highness. You graciously invited me to join you in a game of basketball a time or two."

Mychale frowned, the effort it took to try to think obvious on his face. "So you're treating me with horse medicine?" he asked.

Abby laughed, filled with relief now that he probably wasn't going to die after all. "No, silly. Gregor is a doctor. A people doctor."

"Not quite," he corrected her. "I haven't completed an internship."

"But you will," she said quickly.

Gregor shrugged and turned back to the patient. "Don't worry. I know a lot about this syndrome. I'm confident I can treat it, even if I'm not a fully licensed physician."

But the prince was looking at Abby. "You went and got the doctor for me, didn't you?"

She hesitated, then nodded. She would have said more if Gregor hadn't been there. She would have reminded him that neither one of them wanted their presence here to be known. She would have mentioned that she didn't want Gregor to know she had the baby with her. These were the dilemmas that had swirled through her mind as she was driving down into the village to look for her old friend. What to do and how to do it? Disaster was lurking for any misstep. She'd known she was risking a lot by driving down into the village. And now that she was trapped here, she had to leave quickly and get as far away as possible.

She'd even considered telling Gregor, if she found him, about Mychale's condition, getting his assurance that he would tend to the prince immediately, and then taking off again for the border. In fact, the use of his car would be a godsend. She could leave it just this side of the line. Someone would surely get it back for him before he even needed it.

She'd pulled the car behind Gregor's family home and gone to his window, the same window she and Julienne had thrown rocks at to get him to come out and join them in their excursions to the chalet. When she'd seen Gregor at his desk, leaning over his work just as he had been as a teenager, her heart had leaped into her throat. It was almost too good to be true. As though it were somehow meant to be.

She'd rapped on his window and he'd looked up. She'd been shocked by the black eye patch, but he'd recognized her immediately. When she'd told him the prince was in trouble at the château, he hadn't asked any questions, but grabbed his black bag and prepared to follow her up the hill.

"You mustn't tell anyone about this," she'd whispered to him. "No one must know that Prince Mychale is here. Or that I am here, for that matter."

"You can count on me," he'd told her, and she'd been completely satisfied. If there was anyone in this world she'd always felt she could trust, it was Gregor.

And now she told the prince the same thing. "You can count on his discretion," she said earnestly. "I'd vouch for him above anyone else I know."

There was a curious look in Gregor's eye, but he didn't ask any jarring questions. "Do you think you're ready to move to the couch?" he said to Mychale instead.

The prince was looking stronger by the moment. "Actually, I no longer feel like the move will kill me outright," he said. "Though I would have said so just a few minutes ago."

"Good. Abby, you take his right arm. I'll take the left."

Abby moved into position to use her body as his crutch and support. He slid his arm around her shoulders and she pressed in against him, concentrating on trying to lift.

"Here you go," Gregor was saying. "Just a few steps…"

Abby glanced sideways at the prince and her gaze cruised over his creamy tanned skin and the day-old stubble of his beard. Something shifted inside her, as though her heart had taken a dive off the high board. She gasped softly, but he was concentrating hard on the journey to the couch and didn't notice. She was flushing again. Luckily both men were involved in something pretty intense and not paying any attention to her.

They maneuvered him onto the couch. The prince sank back with a groan, eyes closed, and lay very still for a few minutes. Gregor waited, watching him. Abby watched him, too, her emotions a confused jumble inside her.

"It's okay," Mychale said at last, his eyes still closed. "I'm coming in for a landing. Steady as she goes."

"Good." Gregor took some small bottles out of his bag. "You need to rest for at least twenty-four to forty-eight hours. I'm leaving you some pills to take once you feel like you can get something down."

"That's still not within my grasp," he muttered, opening his eyes into slits.

"It will be in an hour or so. They're just muscle relaxants and a mild diuretic. Take one each, with water. I'll be back in the morning to see how you're doing."

Mychale looked up wryly, wincing against the light. "Thanks, Gregor. I appreciate it."

The doctor nodded. "Not a problem. Abby will take care of you until I come back."

"Will she?"

The prince was looking at her and she knew she looked torn. She was supposed to be over the border by now. He'd wanted her gone, hadn't he? And she'd come around to the feeling that she needed to be gone as far from him as she could get. That surely hadn't changed.

Or had it? His whispering, "Stay" to her a half hour ago still echoed in her mind. The way he'd said it had been a heartfelt request—not a royal order, and it had touched something deep inside her. But she knew he probably didn't even remember saying it.

Still, it was a request she couldn't ignore. Even though it put her plans at risk, she would help him. She knew she couldn't do anything else.

"Of course I will," she said quickly. "I'll be here as long as you need me."

Gregor was looking at her curiously and she knew he was wondering what her relationship with the prince could possibly be. She wished she could tell him it was nothing—nothing at all, just a coincidence that they had both ended up in this gloomy old place at the same time. But answering that question would only bring on a flock of others. Better to bite her tongue and keep the truth to herself.

"Good," he said. "He'll need help and monitoring at least twenty-four hours. This syndrome sometimes comes back in temporary spurts for a while." He looked at the prince. "I'll bet you've been at sea recently," he noted.

Mychale stared at him. "How did you know? I just spent a week cruising."

Gregor nodded. "That's what usually stirs it up, in your family, anyway. Is this the first time you've had it?"

"Yes." Mychale frowned. "Are you saying this a hereditary thing in the royal family, like hemophilia in others?"

"That's right."

"But…how do you know that?"

Gregor hesitated, looking almost embarrassed. "I did my thesis in diagnosis theory on the Montenevadas unique medical history. So you see, I know a lot about it."

The prince was still frowning and there was a touch of suspicion lurking in the look he gave Gregor. "Interesting."

"Your father was prone to Ménière's in his twenties. Then he took up yachting and had a few episodes of the same thing you've got now."

Mychale blinked. "I think I remember that," he said slowly.

Gregor nodded again. "I…well, I just wanted to reassure you that I know what I'm doing," he said. "Even though I'm not fully qualified to practice."

The prince managed a halfhearted smile. "Okay, then. You can practice on me all you want. You've got my vote. I really thought I was going to die." He grimaced. "In fact, dying was looking good there for a while."

"Yes, it's a particularly miserable ailment." Gregor looked from the prince to Abby and back again. "Well, I'll be back tomorrow. Abby will keep watch on your condition and she can drive down and get me if anything goes wrong in the meantime." He flashed her a quick smile. "I'll let myself out. I know the way."

Of course he did. She bit her lip as he left the room, then looked at Mychale to see if he'd noticed that last statement, but the prince was wondering about something else.

"How did you get him up here?" he was asking her.

She gave him a tight-lipped smile. "I drove down to his house. I took your car."

He considered her for a moment. "Did anyone see you? Or notice my car?"

She shook her head. That was just what she'd been so afraid of. Anyone spotting the car would have known it was an unusually luxurious model for this area. Heads would have turned.

"No. His house is in the foothills, on the outskirts of town, before you get to the main residential section. I didn't see another car the whole time, and I parked behind his house and sneaked up to his window to get his attention."

His gaze had a faintly cynical look. "Sounds like that's something you had some experience doing," he said softly.

Her chin rose. She wasn't going to deny it. "In fact, I had. We were mates in the old days."

"Lovers?" he asked softly, watching for her response.

Her eyes widened with outrage. "Good grief no! We were children."

That seemed to please him for some reason. "I take it he was one of your little housebreaking gang," he said.

She sighed, making a note to herself never to assume he hadn't noticed something. He seemed to see all too much. "He was," she admitted.

"In fact, the ringleader."

She hesitated, though she'd always said that she

wasn't sure if that was entirely true. Gregor and Julienne seemed to egg each other on in some ways. As the younger sister, she had pretty much followed along with their wild schemes. But she didn't think there was any profit in going over old history, and she turned, ready to tell him so, but the words stuck in her throat. He might have been a seriously stricken man, but the way he was looking at her belied it. There was an edgy, smoldering sense to his gaze as it seemed to caress her. She caught her breath, not sure if she was reading him right. Was that look really meant for her? Or was her imagination running wild?

"Uh, if you can do without me for a few minutes, I'm going to go check on the baby," she said quickly.

She didn't wait for an answer, and it wasn't until she was out of the room that her shoulders began to relax and she realized how tense she'd been through all this. Things were not going according to plan. In fact, they weren't even going according to the new plan that had taken over for the old plan. It seemed there was a flaw in her basic planning structure somewhere along the line.

"Back to the drawing board," she muttered as she hurried to tend to Brianna.

CHAPTER FIVE

PRINCE MYCHALE slept deeply for most of the night, then fitfully for a couple of hours and when he finally woke, he was feeling like a man with a bad headache rather than a man plunging into the abyss. All things considered, that was quite an improvement.

But lying around for so long had left him in need of some essential maintenance. He contemplated getting up. He still felt quite shaky, but he gritted his teeth and swung his legs off the couch, sitting carefully.

"Hold it," Abby said, coming in from the back of the house. "What do you think you're doing?"

He gave her a baleful look. "There are some things even you can't assist me with," he noted dryly.

But she came up and helped him to his feet anyway. "Lean on me," she ordered.

"I can do this on my own," he replied, resisting.

She looked at him. He was royalty and she should take that into account when he gave an order. But she had experience helping her uncle with patients and she knew illness usually changed everything.

"You're probably right, but you might as well use me

as a backup where you can," she said crisply, positioning herself as his crutch again, setting herself up as the disinterested health worker rather than anything else he might have in mind. At least, she hoped that was the way things would be.

He didn't reply and she couldn't see acceptance in the expression on his face but she held firm. He came all the way to his feet and closed his eyes, stabilizing himself. She moved in closer, helping him.

"How do you feel?" she asked, trying to hide the anxiety she felt. He didn't look all that good and he was leaning on her heavily. But he did have a half smile when he opened his eyes again and looked down at her.

"Dizzy," he said. "But just normal dizzy. Not 'the world has come to an end and I'm spinning in space' dizzy. This I can handle."

His arm was around her shoulders and she was beginning to get well acquainted with his body. What had happened that first night on his bed was just a preview that she'd been too jumpy to appreciate at the time. Now, as she helped him across the room, she had ample opportunity to take in the wonderful maleness of him.

His open shirt revealed smooth, caramel-colored skin covering muscles whose hard-swelling strength surprised her. He looked long and lean. He felt hard and strong. And the feel of his solid flesh was setting up a sensual sizzle inside her that would have set her back on her heels if she'd let it.

"This is as far as you go," he told her at the door to the bathroom. "I'll take it from here."

"Are you sure?" she asked, but she was backing away quickly, glad for a moment to steady herself and get away from the crazy effect he had on her equilibrium.

"I'm sure." He closed the door and she sighed, turning away.

He did need her, and that was just the problem. She couldn't leave while he was still so weak. She'd spent a relatively sleepless night, what with coming out to check on him periodically and then spending some time feeding Brianna and then walking her when she cried.

She'd been so worried, even when she had some time to herself, she couldn't really get any deep sleep. The usual black magic that made everything look hopeless past midnight had been working and she'd been sure he was dying a time or two. She'd crept close and made sure he was still breathing, her heart thudding with fear. And now the dull, heaviness of lack of sleep weighed on her.

Walking to the window, she looked out on the morning gloom. The rain had stopped, but the sky still threatened. There was a break in the weather perfect for a getaway. But she couldn't go.

Why not? She closed her eyes and let her head fall back, agonizing. What was keeping her here? She didn't have any ties to Prince Mychale. She had no responsibilities toward him. No guilt, either, though people would think so once they knew about the claim that Brianna was Crown Prince Dane's missing baby.

The claim was a lie, but there wasn't much chance that she would be able to prove it. Not when her uncle, as royal physician, held all the cards. Her only hope was to get out of the country as fast as she could. So why was she lingering here? A sense of urgency to run for it was eating away at her. But how could she go when the prince needed such a basic level of help?

"Stay," he'd said. Well, she was.

"Lucky you were here to go for the doctor yesterday," he noted as she guided him back onto the couch a few minutes later. "If it weren't for you, I'd probably still be lying on the floor, waiting to die."

She winced at that. "I didn't get the impression the ailment was necessarily life-threatening," she responded, pulling a blanket up over his legs and wondering if that were true. She'd said it more to reassure him than anything—and she certainly hadn't believed it during the night. "And I'm sure someone in your entourage would have shown up eventually."

"Not when they don't know I'm here."

It was something of a relief to know he really didn't expect company, but she wasn't sure she could trust it. She stood back and looked at him.

"How can you just disappear from sight like this?" she asked, perplexed. "I mean, don't you people usually have secret service agents or someone who holds doors and hands you change for the vending machines? Who let you slip your leash like this?"

"I don't need a keeper." He grimaced, realizing his tone was too harsh. "Sorry," he said gruffly. "But this is a fight I've had a few times lately. We spent years not having to put up with that nonsense, living in exile as we did and slinking in and out of various locations. Now they want me to start taking flocks of bodyguards wherever I go."

She considered him, head to the side. "A bodyguard would have helped you more quickly than I did," she noted. "Maybe that's not such a bad idea."

He shrugged. "You did great. I don't need anyone else."

His gaze met hers and she suddenly found herself breathless. What a thing to say! She knew what he meant, but the way he said it made it almost sound as though there was something romantic between them. Just the thought of that was out of bounds. It made her just a little crazy. The memory of the way he had whispered, "Stay," flashed into her mind again. At the time, it had seemed to express a need torn from the depths of his soul, and just thinking about it set up a strange sense of yearning in her heart. She flushed, then turned away, wanting to hide her face from him.

"Did you have any trouble driving my car?" he said, helpfully changing the subject.

"Your car?" For her, this was out of the frying pan and into the fire. She stayed where she was, looking out the huge glass window and avoiding his gaze. If he only knew how terrified she'd been behind the wheel of that fancy monster.

"Oh. A little. But I managed."

He frowned, not sure he liked the way she'd reacted to his question. "You didn't do anything to it, did you?"

She tried to smile and failed miserably. There had been some pretty ugly noises when she'd changed from Reverse to Forward. "I…I don't think so."

"Good." He settled back again. "She's sweet, isn't she? Best car I've ever had."

"Really?" She glanced toward the kitchen, looking for an escape.

"Didn't you think so? How did driving it compare to what you're used to?"

Oh well. Her shoulders slumped. She'd tried to shield him from the truth but if he was going to keep prodding her for input, he was going to have to know. She turned back resolutely and looked him in the eye.

"Actually, I'm not used to much. I don't drive. Not usually."

He blinked, mouth slightly agape. "You…you don't drive?" A look of pure horror flashed from his eyes.

"No. I don't have a license." She hesitated, watching the emotions chase each other across his face. He really did care about this. "In fact, the only car I've ever even tried to drive was my uncle's old stodgy Mercedes, and that was only once and it didn't work out too well." She grimaced. "They said I did something called—was it stripping the gears?"

A strangled sound came from the prince.

"But don't worry, I don't think I did that to your car." She shook her head, remembering the panic that had come into her heart as she'd slid into the driver's seat and looked at the controls. "Your car was like being in a spaceship compared to that. It took me forever just to figure out how to turn it on."

What little color he'd had drained away.

"It's a Lamborghini," he said in a voice like shattered glass. "Custom made for me."

Men and cars. It was a love affair she couldn't fathom. Funny, though—she was almost enjoying torturing him like this. She'd had no idea she had such a cruel streak to her character. That was something she might have to work on in the future. But for now, she rather liked it.

"It's probably fine," she protested with feigned innocence. "I know I got it a little muddy, but I didn't hit anything." She paused for effect, as though thinking back over that hellish drive. "I don't think," she added two beats later, scrunching her nose.

He groaned out his agony and she grinned.

"Oh, your car is fine," she said, getting a little impatient. "I didn't hurt it. It's you we're worried about. How are you feeling and how long do you think you're going to feel this way?"

He started to answer her candidly, then stopped, giving her a steady look as she paced the carpet around him. "Why?" he asked. "Have you got somewhere to go?"

She looked at him sideways. "Well, actually…"

"Sit down."

She turned in surprise. "Why? I'm fine right here."

"Sit down," he ordered, and she sat down in the chair across from him, a pure reflex reaction.

He frowned at her. "I'm getting the feeling you're about to run out the door."

She moved restlessly, her gaze skittering toward his and then away. She couldn't give him the slightest hint as to why she desperately needed to get out of the country. He was a very sharp guy, for a royal. He would figure it out fast, put two and two together, and know she was up to something illegal and possibly even immoral. What then? Would he stop her? Of course he would—and probably have her prosecuted for kidnapping and who knew what else. He was a representative of the law of the land after all, even beyond what he would feel for his brother.

"Well, I do need to leave," she said stoutly, not even

trying to explain why. "You wanted me to go. Remember?"

His eyes narrowed. "That was then. This is now."

That was exactly what she was afraid of.

"Actually I decided you were right," she told him earnestly. "I really need to get going toward my destination. In fact, I was packed and mostly on my way when I found you on the floor. If it hadn't been for that, I would be long gone by now."

"Where were you going?"

She stared at him. She wasn't prepared for that one. She couldn't tell him the truth. "Where was I going?" she echoed limply, looking at the wall. "Uh…"

"You've got nowhere else to go," he said in an infuriatingly all-knowing way. "You might as well stay here."

She was working on a good rejoinder when she realized he wasn't really paying attention any longer. His eyes had a blank look and he was shivering.

"What is it?" She jumped up and went to him without a second thought, putting her hand on his forehead. There was no fever. "Mychale, what is it? Are you cold? I'll get you blankets."

Turning, she ran to the closest bedroom and pulled a big, fluffy comforter off the bed, running back as fast as she could. Her heart was beating wildly. He was still very sick and here she was acting like it was about time he got up and made himself useful to the world.

"Here you go," she murmured, tucking the comforter in around him. "Is that better?"

He didn't answer. His eyes were closed. The shivering slowed, and in a moment she was pretty sure he'd fallen asleep. She breathed a sigh of relief, then crumpled into a heap in the chair as she realized how sick he really was. She wasn't going anywhere. She couldn't leave him. Dread began to spread through her system. She was caught in a trap.

But more than that, she was worried about him. Looking over at where he lay, pale and miserable, her heart twisted. What if this was something more dangerous than they'd thought? Did Gregor know what he was doing? She looked at the clock. Where was he, anyway? She wished he'd set a firm time as to when he would return.

And then she had another thought. What if he didn't come back? What if he'd heard about the missing baby and began to wonder…?

No, Gregor wouldn't do anything to hurt her. She was almost positive about that. Almost.

Prince Mychale stretched and groaned and looked around the room impatiently. He still felt like death, but he was sick and tired of being on this couch. Not only that, he wanted to see Abby, but he was damned if he was going to call for her like a sick child. He closed his eyes and another face swam into view. Stephanie Hollenbeck.

Oh, yes. That little issue he'd come here to find a way to deal with. In all the turmoil, he'd almost forgotten. Here he was, weak as a kitten and feeling incapable of doing anything at all. The Stephanie problem was looming large and seemingly insoluble. Was it useless to try?

"Life is a play," his cousin Nadia always said. "We were given these roles and we've got to perform them to the hilt or be deemed failures. You've got to reach out for those back seats every time."

He wasn't so sure about that, but he did know he didn't much like the part he'd been given. In fact, if he could figure out how to turn it in for a new one, he planned to do just that.

Most of his friends were envious. "Stephanie Hollenbeck?" his friend Jeremy had said plaintively when he heard about the betrothal. "Well there you go. I guess you have to be a prince of the realm to win a woman like that."

Yes, she was beautiful. Exceptionally beautiful. She was also cruel and heartless with ice water where her lifeblood ought to be. The more he got to know her, the more he considered her one of the butterfly people who flittered from one party to the next and never did anything more strenuous than changing the color of their nail polish. She didn't seem to have a worldview beyond the end of her pretty nose. Life revolved around things that might make her happy and that was about it.

The last straw had been when he'd witnessed her embarrassing a little maid on the yacht. The obvious satisfaction she got from the maid's humiliation sickened him. That scene was the catalyst that had rocketed him off into the night, and getting as far away from the woman he was supposed to take as a bride as he could, as fast as he could, became his main goal.

This was the woman he'd promised he would marry? How could he be tied for a lifetime to a woman like this?

"You don't have to live with her," his brother, Crown Prince Dane had assured him from the first. "It's like a business arrangement. We need her father's political support, and his money comes in pretty handy as well."

It had seemed fairly simple the way Dane put it. But

that was before he'd spent a week with her on a yacht in the Mediterranean. To know her was not to love her. And to think of this beautiful ice queen as the mother of his royal children was gag inducing.

Groaning aloud, he threw his head back. How had he let himself get into this situation? He'd promised to marry a woman he couldn't stand.

"Are you okay?"

He opened his eyes and a smile came onto his face. Abby. Now there was a contrast. She could increase the contentment level just by walking into a room. Why couldn't Stephanie be more like Abby?

"I'm fine," he said, turning his head to look at her and then wincing from the blinding pain. "Well, not fine exactly. But I'm still alive. That ought to count for something."

"Who's Stephanie?" she asked.

He looked at her sharply. Had he said the name aloud? Surely he hadn't called it out in his sleep. Unless he'd been having nightmares.

"Stephanie?" he repeated, playing for time. "Why?"

She came closer and he scanned her pretty face. Her look was such a delightful mix of simple elegance and youthful candor, like a fashion model with a scattering of freckles on her nose.

"Because you were muttering her name," she was saying. "Is it Stephanie Hollenbeck? Isn't it true you're going to marry her?"

So she'd heard the news. He supposed everyone had heard by now. It was probably in the papers. Still, to hear that she knew gave him a sick feeling in the pit of his stomach.

"Soldiers who decide they don't want to go into battle and run across the border, seeking asylum are called deserters," he said softly. "What do you call men who don't want to get married?"

The smile that started in her eyes spread to her pretty mouth. "Shirkers," she said firmly. "And they send the authorities after them, too. So take it like a man and keep your commitments."

He groaned, shaking his head as he looked at her. "Et tu, Brute? Don't I have anyone in my corner?"

"Why are you marrying her if…?"

"We each have to do our duty to advance the welfare and prosperity of the country. Part of my job."

She hesitated and a bit of doubt peeked through in her dark eyes. "I know you've got quite a reputation as a playboy prince," she began, "But I think you should consider…"

"Enough." He held up a hand, stopping the words in her throat. Anger flashed in his blue eyes. He was not going to sit here and defend himself against the charge of being a playboy, and he resented it coming from her like he hadn't resented anything in years. Was this the way the country was going to think of him forever? That thought was a knife through his heart.

She waited a moment, then cleared her throat. "Okay, I just want to say one thing," she said, looking as though she might run like a rabbit if he yelled "enough" again. Still, she was going to have her say. "You will have to marry sometime. And have children. As you say, that's part of your job as a royal. And…"

He made a sound low in his throat and she jumped, but she went on, hurrying her words.

"I want you to know that you had a very nice touch with the baby yesterday. I think you'll be a great dad." She took a deep breath and shrugged guilelessly. "That's all."

He stared at her. She couldn't have said anything more out of line with his image of himself. And at the same time, her saying it touched him in a way he would never have dreamed he could be touched. Babies. Not likely.

He wanted to kiss her. The feeling came over him like a warm tropical breeze. Her mouth looked hot and delicious with its rosy bee-stung lips and way her white upper teeth caught hold of the lower lip when she was thinking. For just a moment he imagined his mouth taking hers, hard, as he pulled her lush body up tight against his. His body reacted with a strong, sensual aching like he hadn't felt in a long time.

Hah. Signs of life after all.

"Once you feel stronger," she was saying, completely oblivious to his new hunger for her, "maybe you'd like to hold Brianna again. Maybe hold her bottle. Get to know her better. Once you see how sweet a baby can be, maybe you'll lose your fear…"

"Fear!" He scoffed. "A baby? You think I'm afraid of a baby?"

"It'll be good practice for you," she went on, ignoring his retort. "Surely you'll have some of your own someday and maybe this will set your mind at ease about it."

Have babies? Of course he would. But he certainly didn't plan on taking care of them himself. Did he?

"I'll have plenty of servants to handle all that," he told Abby blithely. "Hopefully I won't ever have to come into direct contact with any of them."

He said the words automatically, a mocking, arrogant retort that he usually wouldn't think twice about making. But everything seemed to be different today. He seemed to be seeing things—including himself—in a slightly different light, from a slightly different angle. And it stopped him cold to realize what he'd just said could have come out of Stephanie's mouth. My God. Was he as bad as she was?

The funny thing was, Abby didn't believe him.

"Now you're just trying to goad me," she said calmly, rolling her eyes.

"Do you really think so?" He wasn't so sure.

"Well, was that how you were raised? Nothing but nannies?"

He blinked, thinking that over. "Not exactly. But the situation was different. We were hiding out in the mountains most of the time. I saw my mother quite a bit, actually. My father was a more distant figure."

"There was a war on," she noted.

He flashed her a quick grin. "Thanks for reminding me."

His grin caused a warm, happy spot to grow in her chest and she quickly left for the kitchen to fix him a little chicken soup. Thinking over what he'd said, she remembered how the royal family had looked to her as a young girl. She'd seen them when they came down into the village. Julienne and Gregor had taken a few trips up the mountain to watch them at play from the outskirts of their estate and come back with tales to tell. All in all, they had seemed a normally happy family to her.

In fact, she and Julienne had been invited up to the

house a few times to attend Princess Carla when there was an official audience with some dignitaries and the regular attendants were missing. They'd both been awed by it all and had liked Carla immensely.

Julienne had felt sorry for her. "She's like a caged bird," she'd noted. "She can't do anything without having it double-checked by everyone."

Abby thought now that she and her sister were soon in the same boat as Carla. Once their parents had died and they'd gone to live with Dr. Zaire, they'd practically been under house arrest. Dr. Zaire's wife, Aunt Winona, still alive in those days, seemed to live in fear of him. Abby and Julienne had rebelled at first, but Dr. Zaire knew how to make punishments so unpleasant one wanted to make sure never to go through it again. The little rebellions had stopped pretty quickly.

And then Julienne had staged the ultimate rebellion for a girl in her position. Abby wasn't even sure how she'd done it. Somehow she'd found a way to sneak out and meet her lover without anyone knowing anything until she was almost in her seventh month.

Abby poured out a small bowl of soup, pulled out a spoon and a small tray and took the makeshift meal out to the prince.

"Do you want to try this and see if you can handle it?" she asked.

Mychale nodded, suddenly ravenous. "Thank you," he said, looking up as she placed the bowl into his hands.

She flushed as though his good manners were unexpected. "You're welcome," she said, sinking into the chair across from where he sat. She sat still, trying not to reveal the restlessness she felt. She had to get out of here. Brianna's future depended on it. But at the same time, where the hell was Gregor? He'd said he would be back today, but he hadn't said a time. She'd assumed it would be in the morning, but here it was, past noon, and no sign of him. What did that mean? Had he decided to look into the royal situation and come up with some suspicions about what she was doing here? He still didn't know about the baby, at least she didn't think he'd noticed Brianna's presence. So what could he possibly suspect? Maybe Mychale was right. Maybe he was selling them out. She didn't want to think such a thing, but if not, where was he?

Mychale ate as much soup as he could manage. The warm liquid nutrition seeped into his body and made him feel almost strong again. He glanced up at Abby. She looked like an angel sitting there with the late afternoon light from the window framing her face. There was a sense of calm about her that he wasn't used to in women. He tried to analyze what it was—and then it came to him. She wasn't coming on to him. Why did every woman he came in contact with want to come on to him?

No, that wasn't actually the way it was. Sure, he knew he was an attractive man, and he knew some women responded to him like a moth to the flame. But most didn't really see him as a man. They saw him as a prince. They saw celebrity and pictures in the tabloids and their name on the lips of the chattering classes everywhere.

That wasn't what Abby saw. He knew that as well as he knew his own mind. He could see it in her eyes.

Troubled eyes. Was she just worried about him, or was there something else nagging at her? He had to think it was the latter. After all, they had never really gotten to the bottom of why she was here in the first place.

"So tell me, Abby," he said coolly, putting aside the bowl. "Who's Brianna's father?" He grimaced as surprise flashed across her face. "I take it the father isn't Gregor."

She shook her head, licking her lips nervously. "I hadn't seen Gregor for almost ten years."

"Then who is it? And why isn't he helping you?"

She drew in a deep breath and tried to think of something to say. She had a quick memory flash of the father's face. She'd only seen him once. Julienne had been so excited about him.

"You've got to meet this guy," she'd said, tugging on Abby's sleeve. "You're not going to believe it."

They were still living in exile at the time, close to the Winter Palace where the royal family was staying. Their uncle's home was a modern penthouse flat decorated in Danish Modern with chrome and glass, rather cold and austere. Julienne couldn't stand it, couldn't stand being confined.

"We might as well be living in an old-fashioned nunnery," she'd fumed. "When do we get to join the twenty-first century, anyway?"

Actually they'd had more freedom there than most of the other places where they'd lived since leaving the lake country. They were in their twenties and eager to burst out of the cocoon Dr. Zaire had kept them in for so long. Julienne begged him to allow her to take drama classes and he'd finally relented. A friend of his ran a small theater in the arts district and he'd promised to keep an eye on her.

Abby wanted to take watercolor classes. Her uncle had waffled for a while and finally decided she was too young to be trusted to deal with artists. Abby had been disappointed, but more than that, she'd been puzzled. What harm would artists do to her?

"Too young!" she'd protested. "Most women my age are already married and having children."

"That's exactly right," he'd told her coldly. "I want to save you for that. You'll thank me in the end. Once we find a suitable match for you, you'll be your husband's responsibility and you'll have all the freedom in the world."

She'd grumbled, but the fact that her uncle had plans wasn't news to her. He'd been talking about it from the day they'd come to live with him, and she knew he was having problems finding just the right men to fulfill his dreams. She and her sister were pretty enough, but they weren't great beauties, as Dr. Zaire was quick to tell them time and time again, and they had no money. They would never attract royalty, and even the second tier of the nobility hadn't shown a lot of interest.

"It's this damn war," he had thundered. "It's ruined everything."

He'd brought in a couple of prospects in recent months, a pair of middle-aged men who had leered at the two of them and fallen asleep right after dinner. Hardly the sort of thing that made a young woman's heart go pitter-patter.

"If this is what it's going to be like," Julienne had whispered to Abby at the time, watching the latest candidate snoring in his dinner chair, "I'd rather be an old maid."

Abby had agreed wholeheartedly, though when

Julienne added, "I think I'll start looking for a lover," she'd been sure her sister was joking.

Whether or not she'd meant it that night, she soon found one.

CHAPTER SIX

"ABBY," Prince Mychale said firmly, "I'm not trying to find out who Brianna's father is. I just want to know why he's not with you."

She drew in her breath and let it out slowly, looking out the window as a stiff wind slashed through the yard like a raiding party, scattering leaves and pinecones as it went.

"He's married," she said simply. "To someone else," she added unnecessarily.

"Abby," he said softly. "I can't believe you would do that."

I didn't! she wanted to cry. But what was the use?

Instead she gave him a flashing glance. "But you don't really know me, do you?" she said shortly. "You don't know what I'm capable of."

"I thought I did," he said, narrowing his eyes as his gaze swept over her. "I thought you were clear as glass, good as gold."

"Think again." Unshed tears stung her eyes and she blinked them back. It seemed only fair to warn him. After all, what she'd done was so much worse than anything he imagined. "I'm a housebreaker, remember? With an illegitimate baby. How good can I be?"

She'd moved too close. Reaching out, he grabbed her wrist and pulled her down to where he was, his grip as hard and strong as it had ever been. She gasped, startled and momentarily confused.

"I don't believe it, Abby," he said firmly. "I look into those dark eyes and I see down to your soul. And what I see…" His voice trailed off.

A smoldering heat seemed to light his eyes. He had her so close, she was drowning in the power of his maleness. She could hardly breathe. The hand she'd used to reach out and stop her fall was flattened inside his open shirt, against his bare chest. She could feel his heart, she could feel his life force, all beneath her touch. She should be struggling to get away. But she wasn't. She couldn't. All she could do was sink further and further into his spell.

And now he was going to kiss her. She was so sure of it, she let her eyelids drift down and her lips part, ready for him, her heart beating like a drum.

But just before his lips found hers, she felt him stiffen and the fingers holding her wrist loosened. When she looked, she saw he was fading into the pull of the illness again. Her heart sank and she reached out to smooth his hair back off his forehead, then drew her hand back quickly and rose, pulling away from him.

What was she doing? He was a prince, for heaven's sake. She had no right to touch him—not now, when he was basically unconscious.

But she stayed there, watching him as he drifted into a restless sleep, wishing she could do something to help him. She could make all the wise crack remarks she wanted to, the truth was, she cared about him. In a strange sort of way, she'd known him all her life. And while that was true, what was even odder was the fact that he didn't know her at all.

Oh, where was Gregor?

She thought about taking the car down into the village again. It was late afternoon and there had been no word from the doctor. Shadows were lengthening. It would be dark soon. Should she go? Should she risk being seen?

She'd been sure she would be gone by now, over the border, heading for safety, Brianna in her arms. And here she was, still tending to a sick prince who would clap her behind bars if he knew what she was up to. Strange world.

He'd seemed better for almost hours at a time, then suddenly seemed worse again in an odd, discomforting way, as though he were going into small comas. That was what scared her. To leave him behind now would be unthinkable. At least, until she got some professional advice.

If Gregor didn't come soon, she was going to have to try driving that terrifying car again. She would wait until dark to lower the risk of being seen in the village. And she would pray that Gregor was still in his house and not on his way to Altamere, the royal palace, to warn them that something was going on out at the summer château.

That was what she feared now. What other explanation could there be that he hadn't come to see about the prince? She spent some time feeding Brianna, played with her and put her back down for a nap, but her mind was on Gregor. If he paid any attention to national events, he had surely heard that there was a baby missing—a baby that was said to be the biological child of the Crown Prince himself. If it had come out that Julienne was claimed to be the baby's mother, he would know there had to be some connection to Abby's mysterious return to the lake country. And since he had such strong affection for and interest in everything the royal family did… Well, it followed, didn't it? That he would run straight to them to tell them what he knew.

By now she'd talked herself into it. She was sure that's what had happened, sure that any moment a caravan of official cars would come racing up the mountain and catch her red-handed. Her mouth went dry as she thought about it. She was sunk. How had she ever thought she could pull this off? She ought to run for it. She had to. She could pull a few things together and be off over the mountain in minutes. After all, she'd gone before. And it had been raining then. This would be so much easier.

Except for one thing. The prince. She thought of him lying on the couch, trying to pull out of this stupid illness, and she knew she couldn't leave him.

"Why?" she asked herself aloud. "Why not? What is he to you?"

That part wasn't really clear. But she knew she couldn't go until she was sure he was all right.

Brianna slept and Abby wandered out into the living room again. Mychale was still sleeping that odd, comalike sleep. She looked down at him for a moment, wondering how she'd come to feel so much affection for a man she could never have. Her gaze traced the hard lines of his handsome face. He was so good-looking, so strong and so wonderful.

And so popular. Ohmigosh. She knew his friends were looking for him right now. They had to be scouring all his old haunts and eventually, they would remember this one. Why was she still here? His entourage would arrive, and then what?

A sound made her look up and when she saw the car approaching from the bottom of the long driveway, her heart stood still for a moment, wondering who it could be.

Gregor! Relief flooded her. Finally. And he seemed to be alone, which was good.

"Where have you been?" she demanded, meeting him at the top of the entry stairs.

"I'm so sorry, Abby," he said earnestly. "But there was an explosion at the trout hatchery. Two employees hurt. I had to accompany them down to the hospital in Taxton and it took all day to get them admitted and settled. I came as quickly as I could."

She searched his eyes, making sure. Was he telling her the truth? She had to think so. He'd never lied to her, but it had been so long since he'd had a chance to.

"I thought you weren't actually licensed to practice," she said.

"True, but I'm all they've got right now. Old Dr. Penne died last spring. It's been difficult finding a replacement for him. So I play the game without the name."

Seeing the look on her face, he mistook it for skepticism about his abilities. "I've passed all the exams, Abby. Don't worry. I know what I'm doing."

"Oh, Gregor, I have no doubt about you," she assured him quickly. She could tell he had some bitterness about the loss of the use of his eye and its effect on his career. Who wouldn't be bitter? But he seemed to be handling it pretty well. And she had to admit, the black eye patch gave him a certain rakish air he hadn't had before. Altogether, he was a very handsome man.

"But I am worried about the prince," she added.

"How is he?" Gregor asked as she led him into the house.

"I don't know." She shook her head fretfully. "He seems pretty normal one minute and then all of a sudden his eyes are sort of rolling back and he slips into a sort of dreamlike state where I can't get through to him anymore."

He nodded. "That can be a part of this ailment. I'm afraid he's got an exceptionally bad case of it. Worse than I thought." He frowned, thinking that over. "He said he'd never had this before. How sure is he of that?"

"You'll have to ask him. I have no idea." She bit her lip. "Do you…do you think we ought to get him down to the hospital?"

Gregor looked at her, head cocked to the side. "Do you want to call in your uncle?" he asked.

"No! Oh, no."

Gregor looked a bit startled by her vehemence.

"He's probably the only other medical professional in the country who has had any experience with this," he pointed out. "As he is the official physician to the royal family."

She looked away, folding her arms across her chest and wishing she knew how much she dared to tell him. "I see."

"And he would know the prince's medical background. There may be something in it I don't know, something that would make a difference."

She nodded, feeling miserable. There you had it. To do this right, they should notify her uncle about what had happened. But if they did that, she and Brianna would be caught. She wanted the best for the prince, but she was already jeopardizing Brianna's future just by being here. She couldn't do any more.

Unless she left. Unless she slipped away and forced Gregor to take over full care of the prince. Could she do that?

"Is that very likely?" she asked uneasily. "I mean that there is something in his medical history you don't know about?"

Gregor gave a short laugh. "No. I've pretty much researched the family from top to bottom. But you never know if there might be something not in the record for some reason."

"Oh."

Gregor stopped and smiled down at her, patting her hand. "Don't worry, Abby. He's going to pull out of this soon. He's going to be fine. Oh, there will be a few more episodes that will scare you. But he'll be okay in the end. As long as I'm right about what he has, of course."

He fumbled with some packages he'd carried in. "I've brought you some food. Bread, cheese and grapes."

"Oh, wonderful."

"And some reading material for the prince once he feels up to it." He handed her two paperback books and a short stack of shiny magazines.

"Good," she said, glancing them over. "There doesn't

seem to be much of a library here. I think they took everything down to the palace when they moved out."

His smile faded and his gaze sharpened. "Well, Abby, don't you think it's about time you told me how you hooked up with the prince?"

"I didn't 'hook up' with him," she disputed hotly. "We just sort of…met along the way and he let me stay here for the night."

He looked skeptical, one dark eyebrow raised. "You're not having an affair with Prince Mychale?"

She looked up at him as earnestly as she knew how. "No, Gregor. I'm not." He hasn't even kissed me, she wanted to say. But she was afraid the regret might show.

He searched her eyes for a long moment. "You know how dangerous that could be, don't you?"

He didn't believe her. She threw out her hands in frustration. "You tell me. You're the expert on the royal family."

"I am, you know. They've always fascinated me, from the time I was very small. When you and Julienne left to go live with your uncle, the royal physician, that intrigued me even more and set me on the course I knew I was meant to take."

"Too bad we couldn't have changed places at the time," she said, trying to make a joke, but her tone sounded tart even to her ears.

He frowned. "Abby, are you in some sort of trouble? Because if you are, I can help you. Just say the word and I'll…"

"No, not at all." Reaching out, she took his hand and smiled at him, a wave of affection plain in her face. "But thank you, Gregor. Julienne and I used to talk about you often. We considered you a sort of honorary big brother, you know. We missed you and the lake country so much."

Her voice broke as she spoke and she wished she'd kept her feelings to herself. But Gregor smiled warmly and squeezed her hand in his.

"I thought of you two as well. When you're ready, I want to hear about what happened to Julienne. I can't tell you how sad it makes me that she's gone." One look at her face and he added hurriedly. "But not now. I understand you're not ready to give me the full story just yet." He sighed. "Shall we go in and see the patient?"

The prince was waiting for them. "I'm really getting sick of this," he warned Gregor, as though the medical man was responsible for it all. "One minute I'm feeling like I could jump up and get back to normal and the next I'm fading into the woodwork again." He moved restlessly. "You've got to give me something to get rid of this. I can't take it much longer."

Gregor sighed. "Believe me, I wish I could. I'm afraid you're just going to have to let this run its course."

The prince swore a long string of soft profanity and Gregor grinned at him.

"That's what I like to hear. The patient getting back that old fighting spirit. Sounds like you've got enough energy to get you to a bedroom for the night. Shall we give it a try?"

"Anything to get off this couch."

"Abby?"

She stepped forward to help with a certain amount of dread. This was getting harder and harder to do. She was so afraid she was going to give herself away if she wasn't careful. Something about this man appealed to her senses like no man she'd ever known had ever done. Of course, she hadn't known a lot of attractive, sexy men of this caliber. She had a feeling this one was enough. Just knowing him could make a woman an expert on the subject.

The downstairs bedroom was close by and she'd prepared it for this very eventuality. The bed itself was huge, but the room was big as well, with heavy drapes framing a huge bay window that overlooked the neglected, overgrown kitchen gardens and gave a broad view of the snow-capped mountaintop beyond. Beautiful antique furniture completed the picture. It was a fine room to use for convalescence. She was sure he would be as comfortable there as he would be anywhere.

Mychale's arm came around her shoulders and his body pressed against hers feeling even more delicious than it had felt before. This time he came across more natural, more alive, thrilling her senses and leaving her afraid both men would hear the way her heart thudded in her throat. Even more embarrassing was the way she was breathing like a long distance runner at the three-mile mark.

Luckily Gregor was talking, going on and on about signs Mychale should be looking out for during his recovery and Abby knew she should be listening and filing this information away, just in case, but she couldn't follow a word he was saying. How could she get her mind to work normally when Mychale kept turning toward her. She avoided his gaze but she could feel his warm breath on her neck. And then he buried his face in her hair and took a long, slow breath, breathing in her scent.

For just a moment, time stood still. Her own breath

caught in her throat, choking her. Something twisted inside her, as though she'd gone over a hill, very fast, and she realized it had to be her heart. Horror swept through her. This was what Gregor had hinted at when he'd warned her of danger. This was the way it would start.

She tried to pull as far away from him as she could, but with his arm around her shoulders, it wasn't an easy task. And finally they were in the bedroom. It was with a great sense of relief that she released her hold on him and let him slide down onto the crisp white sheets of the king-size bed. Then she stood looking at him for a long moment, catching her breath and calming her heart rate.

Gregor was still talking as he went back to the living room for his supplies but she didn't think Mychale was listening any more than she was. He was watching her, his blue gaze holding hers as though he could cast spells.

"I could have made that on my own, you know," he told her softly.

Try as she might, she couldn't pull her own gaze away. "Then why didn't you?" she whispered back.

He didn't answer but his sensual smile told her everything she needed to know—everything she already knew—and she flushed, finally gathering strength to turn away as Gregor returned, hoping that her old friend wouldn't notice the effect the prince had on her.

It was scary, but she had to admit, it was thrilling at the same time—like nothing she'd ever known. Her blood was still singing in her veins and excitement sizzled on her skin. Just being with the prince was intoxicating. Having him flirt with her could be devastating if she wasn't careful.

A thought flashed into her head. What would Julienne

Play the *Lucky Hearts* Game

and get...

2 FREE BOOKS and 2 FREE MYSTERY GIFTS...

YOURS to KEEP!

yes! I have scratched off the silver card. Please send me my *2 FREE BOOKS* and *2 FREE mystery GIFTS* (gifts are worth about $10). I understand that I am under no obligation to purchase any books as explained on the back of this card.

Scratch Here!

then look below to see what your cards get you... 2 Free Books & 2 Free Mystery Gifts!

316 HDL ESRM   **116 HDL ESUX**

FIRST NAME

LAST NAME

ADDRESS

APT.#

CITY

STATE/PROV.

ZIP/POSTAL CODE

(H-R-09/08)

Twenty-one gets you
2 FREE BOOKS and
2 FREE MYSTERY GIFTS!

Twenty gets you
2 FREE BOOKS!

Nineteen gets you
1 FREE BOOK!

TRY AGAIN!

Offer limited to one per household and not valid to current subscribers of Harlequin Romance® books. All orders subject to approval.
Your Privacy – Harlequin Books is committed to protecting your privacy. Our Privacy Policy is available online at
www.eHarlequin.com or upon request from the Reader Service. From time to time we make our lists of customers available to
reputable third parties who may have a product or service of interest to you. If you would prefer for us not to share your name
and address, please check here. ☐

have made of this scene? She could only imagine her sister's eyes lighting up with mischievous joy.

"See Julienne?" she thought, feeling as though she'd been drinking champagne. "I can generate a little male interest myself." And that made her smile.

Oh, she did miss her sister. If only she'd known what Julienne was up to in time to protect her better. If only she'd noticed and done something to stop her.

But she hadn't guessed that her sister had taken to walking on the wild side of life until it was much too late. At the time she first began making those restless, provocative suggestions, Abby had done the only thing she could think of to do—spun castles in the air, promising Julienne that they would run away together to the coast and find a little cottage to share and find their own men.

Her sister hadn't bought into it. "The only cottage at the shore we could afford would be a dump and the only men hanging around a dumpy part of the beach would be grizzled old fishermen or those weirdos with metal detectors. I want to have fun. I want to live. And I want it now!"

Julienne had always been the impatient one, the one who couldn't wait. She'd reached out and grabbed life. And life had sunk its teeth in her neck.

Abby shuddered, wishing she hadn't come up with such a disturbing picture. But it did seem as though her sister had been punished for doing what so many other young women got away with every day. She'd only wanted to fall in love.

When Abby had realized what was going on, she'd tried to reason with her sister.

"Julienne, if Uncle catches you…!"

"What's he going to do? Cut off my Saturday morning cartoons? He still thinks I'm a child."

They both knew he had the power to do a lot more than that. In fact, he'd been getting increasingly erratic. The death of the old king had thrown him into a state of severe melancholy for a long time, and when he'd come back out of it, he'd gone into a frenzy of activity, most of it seeming to try to ingratiate himself with the royal family that was left. And that was odd, because she knew for a fact that he despised the princes, thought them a group of lightweights and slackers.

She looked at Mychale, his body hard and tanned as he lay back against the white sheets while submitting to Gregor's blood pressure cuff and various other tests. This was no slacker. The more she got to know him, the more she realized he had depth and character that she wouldn't have expected in a royal.

She caught herself up short. Admiring the prince was all right. Even liking him. Maybe. Just don't fall for the man, she told herself sternly. You might as well throw yourself off a cliff as do that.

"You seem to be coming along all right," Gregor said at last, beginning to pack his things away in his black bag. "I'm a little concerned that you still go into short periods where you seem to lose consciousness." He turned to Abby. "You're going to have to watch him full-time tonight. I'll let you use your own judgment, but you should consider letting me know immediately if he seems to be losing consciousness for longer than an hour at a time."

Abby frowned, not sure she understood. Glancing at the prince, she noted that he seemed a bit puzzled as well. "You want me to check on him every…?"

"No," Gregor interjected. "I want him watched consistently. I think it would be best if you slept here in the room with him."

Abby gasped and looked quickly at Mychale. A slow, pleased smile was beginning to make its way from his eyes to his entire handsome face. He tried to hide it, but without much success. Clearing his throat, he put on an air of calm deliberation.

"Let me get this straight," he began, attempting to hide the cat-that-ate-the-canary grin. "I'll be in danger if Abby…uh, if someone isn't constantly checking to see if I've fallen into a sort of coma. Is that right?"

"Something like that," Gregor said, seemingly oblivious to the crackle of sensual tension he had lit off in the room. "I am worried that you might begin to fall into a pattern that can start spiraling out of control. I think the monitoring needs to be nonstop, just in case. Abby will have to bring some bedding in and put together something makeshift on the floor or maybe on the love seat. She can set a clock to let her wake periodically and check if your breathing is normal. But it would be best if she was right here where she could notice any irregularities immediately. Your breathing is important."

"Ah, yes. My breathing." Mychale managed a wise look, nodding as he looked at Abby. "I definitely want that kept under control."

She hardly knew what to think. She was still in state of shock.

Gregor glanced at her apologetically. "Sorry to ruin your night like this," he said. "But I really will feel better if someone monitors the situation, at least for tonight."

"Oh. No problem," Abby said, her voice strained as

her gaze skittered around the room without finding anything safe to stick to. "I just wish you would be a little more explicit as to what I'm to watch out for."

"Come with me," he said, turning briskly. "I'll jot down the warning signs you should be looking for."

"All right," she said faintly, following him out.

At the door she paused and looked back, wide-eyed. Mychale was still smiling and he gave her the most lurid wink she'd ever seen. She got in one quick glare before turning to join Gregor, but she was moving in a haze of disbelief. She'd just been given an assignment to spend the night with the prince. And from the very man who'd warned her against emotional entanglements with royalty. This was insane.

Abby wasn't sure what to expect when she came back into the bedroom with two flashlights and her bedding folded over her arms after Gregor had gone back down to his home. What she found was the prince frowning moodily, all signs of their recent sense of awareness gone. To say the least, she was surprised.

But it gave her a moment to look him over while she drew the drapes tightly around the windows and set up the small battery-run lantern they would use as darkness fell. She was searching for signs of recovery and there were plenty of them. His eyes were bright and the way he held himself, leaning back against the headboard, propped by pillows, showed a return to control and strength that had been missing for the last twenty-four hours. He was much better. There was no doubt about it. That gave her a quick sense of relief.

But as she looked more closely, she detected a tightening around his eyes, a taut, stretched look to his skin, a strained look to the way he was balanced, that showed he still had a long way to go to full health.

"Abby, tell me this," he said without preamble, fixing her with a steady gaze from those brilliant blue eyes. "I know that you've said that you trust Gregor implicitly. Why? And why should I trust him?"

She set the linens down on a chair and turned to consider his question, her head to the side.

"He's my oldest friend," she said slowly, thinking. "His father worked for your family for years. He's never done anything to cause you suspicion. That I know of. Why shouldn't you trust him?"

"Why shouldn't I trust him?" He repeated the question as though it were too naïve for words. "Abby, I can't afford to take anything on faith."

She shrugged. "What about me?" she asked simply.

"You." The hard look in his eyes softened and his gaze caressed her face. "You're different."

"Am I?"

He waved the question away. "Of course. You probably saved my life."

"Oh, I did not."

He nodded. "Gregor said I could have had irreparable damage if you hadn't gone for help when you did."

"Well, it's lucky that didn't happen." She smiled and shrugged. "But it's more thanks to Gregor than to me."

His eyes darkened. "Here's the problem. About Gregor." He hesitated as though not sure if he really should be telling her this, but in a few seconds he seemed to make the decision to go on. "I've got to tell you, I can't trust anyone who's got this much of a fixation on the royal family. He did his thesis on our diseases. Who knows what else he's studied about us? Don't you find it all a little strange? Motive comes into play. You have to wonder just what is going on with this guy."

Abby felt a chill shiver down her spine. After all, she'd had moments of similar doubts. But she wanted to deny them. "He's helping you and he's keeping our presence here secret. Isn't that evidence of good intentions?"

"So far so good. We'll see." He still looked troubled. "I'm just warning you to be ready for anything."

She stared at him. What could he possibly mean? He was talking as though they were a team, as though any threat to him was a threat to her. That didn't really comport with reality. What was he thinking?

"Being royal means you're always prepared for those closest to you to try to sell you out," he said softly, searching her gaze with his own. "Would you lie to me, Abby?"

Her heart sank. *Oh, Mychale, if you only knew!*

"I may be lying to you already," she answered crisply. She bit her tongue. She shouldn't have said that. And so she added quickly, "But regardless, please believe that I would never do anything to harm you."

He stared at her for a long moment, then the corners of his mouth twitched. "That's supposed to reassure me?" he thundered at her at last, half-laughing. "'Hey, I may sell you out, but I'll only do it out of my deep respect for you.'" He shook his head, disgusted. "Where have I heard that one before?" he muttered.

"That's not what I meant," she protested.

"Maybe that wasn't what you said," he told her. "But it's what I heard."

"Then I suggest you clean out your ears," she said airily. "I'm going to get Brianna. I'll be right back."

"Whoa," he said, stopping her in her tracks. For just a moment it looked as though he were ready to leap up out of bed to stop her. "Hold on. Why are you getting the baby?"

She looked at him, her chin high. She'd wondered when he was going to tumble to the fact that Brianna was part of this deal. "Because she's going to sleep here, too. I won't leave her alone in another part of the house."

He stared as though the whole idea had left him thunderstruck. "You're kidding," he said at last.

"No, I'm dead serious. I won't stay here if she doesn't."

Her pulse began to race. She was taking chances here. She knew she wasn't going to leave him to his own devices for the night. But she wasn't going to do that to Brianna, either. If he called her bluff, she would have to sleep in the hallway. With the baby at her side.

"That's crazy," he said curtly. His gaze was fierce as it raked over her. "Babies cry and get dirty diapers and generally make life miserable and you can't deny it."

Her chin came up defiantly. "Babies are part of life. Deal with it."

His eyes narrowed as though he could hardly believe she was making such a silly argument. "You can't sleep in the same room with babies," he declared resolutely. "It's not civilized."

She tossed her hair back over her shoulder. "Then call me a savage."

His jaw hardened stubbornly. "I don't want a baby here."

Her eyes flashed. "Then you won't have me here, either." She was trembling slightly, but she stuck to her guns. "Your choice."

Their gazes met, clashed and held—and held longer. Abby was determined not to drop her gaze first, even if she could hardly breathe. His gaze was a force, even in his weakened state. She felt seared, like a sentinel being blasted with a whirlwind. But she stood her ground.

His gaze didn't falter, but at last he said, "Does she sleep through the night yet?"

Abby almost went limp with relief and she smiled because she knew she'd won the battle. "Sometimes." She could afford to be magnanimous in victory. "Don't worry. I'll take her out of the room if she gets fussy. I'm not doing this to torture you, you know."

He grunted. "You could have fooled me," he muttered. "I'm not sure I can sleep with a baby in the room."

"Sure you can. They're people, too."

"Of a sort," he grumbled.

"A very good sort," she responded cheerfully. "I'll just go get her."

"You do that," he muttered, watching her go, dreams of a night alone with Abby evaporating before his eyes. Too bad.

And he was feeling much better. In fact, if anyone had asked him, he would have said he didn't see why he needed monitoring during the night. But once he'd understood what was going to be involved, he'd decided any excuse to get Abby closer was a good deal.

He liked Abby. He liked her a lot. She had an odd effect on him. On the one hand, her presence was soothing and reassuring. He felt calmed and comforted just hearing her pass by where he was lying. But at the same time, her pretty face and luscious body turned him on in ways he didn't remember being turned on before.

He was used to women whose whole raison d'être was generating the "must have some of that" libidinous reaction in men and to tell the truth, he'd grown jaded lately. Voluptuous ladies with breasts spilling out of their cocktails gowns and artificially enhanced lips swelling as though a herd of rogue bees had just passed through the area were boring. Too obvious. Too class-less. He wasn't a boy any longer. He was a man and he wanted a woman who knew how to grow in character and intellect. Like Abby.

Of course, it didn't hurt that she was cute as hell.

Her baby, on the other hand, seemed to be mostly a nuisance. He had vague memories of holding her the day before, just prior to his collapse. That hadn't been so bad, but he certainly didn't want to repeat it. Babies had their place, that place just wasn't in his life.

He was sounding arrogant and insensitive again. Too bad. He was a royal, damn it. He was supposed to be a bit autocratic. People expected it.

So why did he regret his occasional high-handed at-titudes when he noticed Abby's reaction to them? He wasn't sure about that. He wanted her approval, natu-rally. He wanted to see her applauding his every action from the sidelines. That was all part of the usual plan. He was attracted to her and he wanted to get her into his bed. He was a normal male, after all.

But disturbingly, there really seemed to be more to it than that. What that meant, he wasn't sure he really wanted to know.

CHAPTER SEVEN

"HERE she is," Abby announced, holding Brianna out for the prince to see. "Isn't she a pretty girl?"

Mychale looked up but his gaze went to Abby first. She couldn't read what he was thinking, but there was something disturbing in his eyes. When he glanced at Bree, it was with a grudging reluctance and she expected the worst. Either he would show downright disdain, which would make her furious, or he would barely notice her, pretend she didn't exist. That would make her mad, too, but she might be able to tolerate it in the short run.

But neither of those things happened. Instead a look of surprise came over his face and he did a double-take, his gaze on Brianna for longer than Abby could ever have hoped.

"Hey," he said, blinking at the baby now resting against Abby's shoulder. "She smiled at me."

"Hmm?" she said skeptically. Abby supposed it was possible, but she was a little young for that. "It was probably gas," she added helpfully, leaning back as she searched the little gamin face and finding no evidence of smiling.

He looked outraged by her skepticism. "Why would it be gas? Haven't you been feeding her right?"

Abby gave him a superior look and refused to comment as she tucked the baby's shirt in around her and propped her up against her shoulder again. Cuddling her close, she patted her back and jiggled a bit, giving her a little ride.

"There," he said. "She did it again."

"Right." Abby gave him a look and just stopped herself from rolling her eyes.

"No, really, that was a smile," he insisted firmly. He was watching her like a hawk now. "Wasn't it, baby girl?" he said.

Abby shifted the burden from one shoulder to the other. Turning quickly, she caught him making faces at the child. She had to laugh.

"You're cheating," she said.

"It's called communication," he countered. "We've got a thing going on here, don't we, little one?"

She looked from the baby to the prince and back again. Brianna gave a little burp, then looked surprised. Mychale laughed aloud and so did Abby, though she still saw no evidence of a smile

"Would you like to hold her?" she offered hopefully.

"Not at all, thanks."

He sat leaning back against the headboard with his hands clasped behind his head, seeming very casual. And also very non-baby-friendly. She stared at him for a moment, feeling rebuffed. She wasn't sure why, but there was an impulse deep down that she couldn't seem to shake—an impulse to convince him that he really did like babies after all.

But why? What did it matter? She had to get over it. It really was none of her business what he liked. He was royal. He could like what he wanted. It had nothing to do with her.

The light from the electric lantern sent eerie shadows against the walls. She paced the room, humming to Brianna to put her to sleep, and all the while she was aware of Mychale watching. His gaze never left her. At first it made her a little nervous, but soon it began to feel good. A warmth was spreading slowly through her body. His interest in her was more and more intoxicating. She liked it. There was no denying it.

Finally Brianna was asleep. Abby settled her carefully into the little bed she'd built out of the drawer. She pulled the blanket up and smiled down at her, admiring her little round cheeks and the long eyelashes making shadows on her face. Her heart so full of love, it brought tears to her eyes.

"Isn't she adorable?" she murmured.

"Adorable?" He said the word as though it was new to him, then looked down at the baby bed. "I suppose. But I was just sitting here thinking you were fairly adorable yourself."

She glanced at him, hoping she could keep from flushing. "Don't be silly."

"Oh, I'm not."

There was something dangerous in his tone, a hint of just how deep his attraction was running at the moment. She blinked and warned herself. This man might be sick, but he was still a man, and a royal one at that. He was used to getting what he wanted when he wanted it.

And wanting something else a few minutes later,

she reminded herself sternly. So don't go getting any grand ideas.

She looked around the room and decided to sit in the antique chair that was closest to the bed. She sat down gingerly, knowing it was old and guessing it was probably valuable. Then she turned and faced him.

"Why don't you like babies?" she challenged straight out.

He stared at her for a moment, then made a face. "The question is irrelevant. I have no interest in babies. There are no babies in my life. What I think about babies is immaterial to anything."

"Untrue," she said. "Your brother, Prince Nico, just married a woman who is about to have a baby. They've been keeping it under wraps, but everybody knows it. So you're going to have a baby in the family. I don't think you're going to be able to ignore that."

He shrugged. "I'll manage to avoid all that as much as possible."

She shook her head, determined to show him just how much she disapproved of his position. "I hope you make some adjustments before you get married," she told him. "Or you could be in for a bumpy ride. I know I couldn't marry a man who didn't want children."

She expected him to point out that he wasn't planning to marry her, so the problem was moot, and she braced herself for it. But he didn't do that. Instead he actually seemed to consider her opinion on the matter.

"You say that now because you pretty much have to, considering." He nodded toward where Brianna slept. "Try to stand back and detach yourself for a minute. Be objective. What real good do babies do anyone? They only stay cute and little for a few paltry years. Then they go on to make your life miserable as adolescents and teenagers. Why would you throw away the possibility of a wonderful relationship with the perfect man for you just because you refused to forgo all that bother and misery in your life?"

She was tempted to go for his last statement first, but she knew he was expecting that, so she countered in a different way.

"So you admit you think they're cute at first, do you?"

"What?" He looked surprised, then a bit sheepish. "Yes, I suppose so."

"Good." She smiled. "It's a start."

He looked at her with humor and laughed. "Abby, you're just so…" He hesitated, a word on his lips, a word he knew he would regret using. But what the hell. "You're just so precious," he said, feeling foolish, but accurate.

She made a face at him, but she colored at the same time and couldn't help but look flattered.

"Well, I guess I'll get ready for bed." She was going back to the maid's room where her nightclothes were still stored. She looked at him. "Do you need any help to…?"

"No," he said firmly. "You get ready your way, I'll get ready mine."

She smiled and gave him a salute. "Aye aye, sir," she said, picking up a flashlight and muting it with her hand as she opened the door.

Ten minutes later, she was back in her yellow night-gown, but also sporting a fluffy robe she'd found in a closet. Mychale was back leaning against the head-board, but this time he was completely shirtless. She stopped in her tracks. If he were naked…!

"Don't worry," he said, forestalling her charge. "I found some pajama bottoms in a drawer. I put them on, just for you."

"Thank you," she said with a heartfelt sigh. "Too bad you only found half of the set."

"This bothers you?" he asked, looking ingenuous.

She opened her mouth to tell him the truth, then shut it again. After all, he'd met her halfway with the pajama bottoms. Maybe it would be a bit churlish to ask for more. And to do so, she would have to admit that it did bother her. And it did. It bothered her very much indeed.

The lantern-light was muted. It cast a golden hue on his skin and shadowed his eyes, turning them black. His chest looked beautiful, like a sculpture, lovingly rendered. A major work of art. He took her breath away.

She tried to keep from looking at him. Instead she worked with the pillow and thick comforter she'd set up in the love seat in the far corner.

"That's too far away," he said, frowning as he watched her. "How are you going to keep track of my breathing from there?"

She looked up, but didn't respond. His mouth was twisted into half a smile. He was teasing her.

"That reminds me," she said, picking up the alarm clock. "What intervals shall we use for the checkups? I think every other hour."

"Forget it," he said bluntly.

"What?" She looked up at him, surprised.

"I'm much better, Abby. Can't you tell? I haven't had a spell for about four hours, and the last one I had was barely a five-minute nap. I'm finished with that."

She shook her head, appalled. "We can't know that. It would be better if I checked."

"Okay, check me out at 3:00 a.m. If there's no sign of any problem, go ahead and sleep the rest of the night."

She frowned and carefully set the alarm for midnight and then for three. "Okay," she said. "Good night."

"Not so fast," he shot back. "Come on over here. We need to talk."

She wanted to claim that they could talk from their respective corners, but she knew that wasn't true. Not if they expected to let Brianna sleep. Reluctantly she made her way to his bedside.

"Come on up," he said, patting the area beside him.

"I don't know," she said nervously. "I'm not sure."

"Look, I promise not to seduce you," he said. Then, with a guileless shrug, he added, "Unless you ask me to, of course."

She took a deep breath, determined not to show weakness. She had spunk. She needed to use that. Her chin rose and she sent him a flashing message with her eyes.

"Not likely," she said, and plopped onto the bed, sitting sideways. "What do we need to talk about?"

His smile was brief and cool. "Now that my head is fairly clear, I think it's time for a full explanation of why you're here and how you got here."

Uh oh.

She picked up a corner of the bedspread and began pulling at the loose threads. There was a very good reason he might feel he hadn't gotten the full story yet. She hadn't given it to him. And she never would. But he wasn't going to be satisfied without a little more meat on the bones. She would have to add a few details.

"I…uh…haven't I explained all that to you?"

"No, you haven't." That autocratic, royal tone was back. "Give it to me straight. From the beginning."

She swallowed. She could do that. She could hit the high points. She just had to be careful not to tell him anything that would send out a warning signal. She would have to weigh her words carefully.

"All right." She turned and looked him in the eye, hoping that would convince him of her truthfulness. "I've told you my uncle was making plans for Brianna that I couldn't abide."

"What sort of plans?'

She paused, heart beating. This was one of those areas she was not going to be able to clarify for him. "I'm sorry, but I'm not going to go into that. Not right now." She licked her lips, noting the hard look that had come into his eyes. But what could she do? The truth would ruin everything at this point. "Suffice it to say, I didn't approve. In fact, I was horrified. But being the sort of man he is, with the sort of power he has over me, I knew I couldn't fight what he wanted to do. Not there while I was in his control."

She looked into his face to see how he was taking this. He looked cool, reserved, but not antagonistic. That gave her a bit of hope.

"So I knew I had to take her away from his sphere of influence. I tried to think of the best place I could go where we could be safe while I thought out my options. I remembered how much I loved it here in the lake country. And I made plans to bring her here." She sighed, remembering how hard it had been to make those decisions, how frightening it had been to take that step.

"I made a reconnaissance mission up here last week to make sure this place was empty and to bring some supplies. Then, a few days ago, I bundled Brianna up, left some travel folders lying around to disguise where I intended to take her and we left. We took a bus to Merdune and then the train up here."

She took a deep breath, as though she'd just finished a difficult task. And then she looked into his gaze again. He was frowning.

"You walked all the way from the station, carrying Brianna?"

"Yes. It wasn't a problem. It was wonderful to be back here in lake country, with Larona down in the valley. It was like coming home. Just breathing in the air…" She stopped, afraid she was going to tear up again.

The whole concept of home was fraught with memories of her parents, of Julienne, of all that had happened lately. Sometimes it felt like a weight on her chest to have the past hanging over her. Sometimes she felt so hopeless.

"Go on."

Taking another deep breath, she continued.

"That's about it. We came here and settled in. I began trying to figure out where we would go next, where we would be safe from my uncle. And then you showed up."

He was quiet for a moment, staring at the wall behind her. "Was he really so bad?" he asked at last. "Was there really no one you could appeal to for help?"

"Yes, he is that bad. And no, there was no one."

He nodded slowly, thinking that over. "I'll be honest," he said at last. "I never understood why my father was so fond of the man. I never liked him much."

She tried to smile. "He doesn't like you, either."

Mychale grunted. "That's disturbing."

"It is," she said earnestly. The truth was out now. Why not tell him? "He rather despises you all." She hesitated. "I take that back. He does like your sister. He was always telling us—my sister Julienne and me—how we should be more like Carla. But not," she added with a short laugh, "not like your cousin Nadia. He was particularly scathing about her."

"Carla's a peach," Mychale murmured.

"Yes."

"But Nadia's pretty wonderful, too. She and I have always been particularly close."

Yes, she knew that. "Actually I know Nadia," she told him. "And your sister Carla, too." She looked at him quickly, remembering that he'd seen her at her birthday.

He nodded. "Were you often at the parties?" he asked, thinking all the time he'd wasted in not getting to know her sooner.

"Not really. But a few years ago, at the winter palace in exile in Dharma, Julienne and I were recruited to fill out the classes that had been set up to teach royal etiquette to both of them. We weren't the only ones. About ten young ladies of various attachment to the royal family attended the classes. We had teas and little dances and things like that. In fact," she added as the memory popped into her mind, "you came to one of the dances. I remember it distinctly."

He smiled. "Did I dance with you?"

"No, not once." She gave him a reproachful look. "You never gave me a glance."

He seemed pained by her revelation.

"But then, I was never the type to attract a lot of male attention," she admitted.

He gave her a slow, crooked grin. "Let's just say you may not be the best judge of that," he said, making her flush again. "Or that you must have changed a lot since those days."

She shrugged. It hardly mattered. "I always liked Carla very much," she said, trying to get the conversation back on track.

"And what about Nadia?"

She hesitated. Should she tell him the truth? Why not. "She was scary."

He laughed. "Yes, she can be scary."

"She was too sophisticated to pay any attention to me. As a matter of fact, now that I think back, she spent most of that dance looking superior in the corner with you." She'd always thought women like Nadia were the sort the prince was drawn to. He had an elegance about him that seemed right in tune with that sort of fashionably dressed woman who seemed wrapped in world-weary mystery. Unlike open, ordinary girls like Abby. She and her sister used to joke that they could never be as interesting as women like Nadia—they just smiled too much.

"Abby…" He took her hand and began to play with her fingers.

"But I always got along very well with Carla," she went on, trying to ignore the fact that her hand was in his possession. "She's very down-to-earth. I like her."

"Everyone likes Carla," he said softly. "She's one of the good ones."

"Yes."

"Just like you."

"No!" She pulled her hand away abruptly. "No, your highness, I'm…I'm not…"

"Abby." He grabbed both her hands and held them in his. "Don't ever call me that when we're alone." The lantern-light caught his eyes at an angle and they seemed to be giving off sparks. "Because, Abby…I'm going to kiss you."

She drew in her breath but she couldn't look away.

"And I want you to kiss me back." His voice was so low, it was almost a whisper. "Not because I'm royal and you think you have to. I want you to kiss me back because you want to." His hands tightened on hers and he pulled her closer. "Is that going to work for you?"

Staring into his silver-blue gaze, she nodded wordlessly, too choked to speak. She couldn't breathe. She couldn't think. She didn't want to think, because she knew if she did, she would make him stop. This was no good, and nothing good could come from it. But right now, she didn't care. She wanted his kiss more than she'd ever wanted anything in her life. The intensity of her need to feel his mouth on hers was like nothing she'd ever known.

She lifted her face to him. He was so close she could feel the heat from his body. He bent closer and then his lips touched hers. She opened to him and gasped as his tongue found hers. He tasted like wine and felt like fire and she surrendered without a shot, closing her eyes and giving herself up to the sensation of a tantalizing tenderness mixed with raw desire.

She'd never experienced anything like this, even in dreams. Her heart was beating so hard, she was afraid it might burst. His hands held her head, framing her face, as though she were indeed something precious, but his mouth was all plunder and exploration. He swept her away from reality, carried her up into a new and thrilling place where she could fly.

She welcomed the warm sensual spell he created, joining him with a sense of discovery, and she knew this was all she wanted. She'd been waiting all her life for this and wanted to stay here forever, lost in his embrace, living for his kiss. When he began to pull away, she moaned low in her throat, following him, wanting more and not ashamed to let him know it.

But Mychale knew she'd had enough. Her response was so open and left her so vulnerable. He pulled back and stared at her, not sure what he'd gotten himself into.

He'd wanted to kiss her. That impulse had been with him from the first. But he'd known the danger it would pose and he'd resisted. Then, sitting here watching her put the baby to sleep, he'd realized he was going to do it—that he wanted to do it—that he wanted a lot more than one simple kiss. So when she'd sat down on the bed beside him, he'd taken the opportunity for what he'd thought would be a moment or two of pure pleasure.

He'd had that. But there had been so much more. She was sweet and pure and willing in a way that set him on fire. And at the same time, there was an innocence to her response, a hesitancy, a lack of experience that stunned him.

As the dull ache of wanting her had quickly become a driving need that had taken all his strength to draw back from, he'd wanted to push away that silly robe and the silky nightgown, to cup her breasts in his hand, to taste their pink tips and send her body into a state of acceptance and demand—a state he could sense was just trembling beneath the surface with her. He'd wanted to pull her down onto the bed and hold her there with his body. Hell, he'd wanted to take her up and make sweet love to her until she cried for mercy.

But a man had to know his limitations. And his responsibilities. And he'd promised not to seduce her. So he'd held it back—but it hadn't been easy. He had to admit, she'd thrown him off balance with her open and charming reaction to the kiss. And as he worked to recapture his equilibrium, she confused him even more.

"Oh my," she was saying breathlessly, her eyes wide with wonder as she gazed up at him. "I…I didn't know…."

He lifted her face with a forefinger under her chin and smiled down at her. "What didn't you know?"

"I…I just didn't know it would be like that." She closed her eyes and shivered. "I've never been kissed that way before."

He stared at her, then looked away. Something wasn't right here. She was too innocent. How could she be this inexperienced and have a child? It didn't make any sense. And yet, how could he ask her about that and put it in a delicate way that wouldn't scare her or make her defensive?

Turning back, he stroked her cheek. She turned her face into the palm of his hand, pressing a quick kiss where his pulse was beating, sending a shock of tenderness through his heart.

"Who's kissed you before, Abby?" he asked her softly.

She laughed low in her throat, still tingling from what they had just shared. "Oh, just a dumb boy in school. And then a man my uncle wanted me to marry."

She shuddered, remembering. "Ugh. That was creepy." She looked up at him and her face changed. "This was heaven and magic and a ride on a wave," she told him candidly, then sighed, half-laughing, looking rueful. "I liked it. I liked it too much."

He dropped a quick kiss on her soft, sweet lips. "I liked it, too," he told her, feeling a wave of warmth for her he didn't remember feeling toward any woman for a long, long time. "But, Abby, you puzzle me. If I didn't know better, I'd say you were completely inexperienced."

Her smile as she looked up at him was radiant. "But I am."

"You are." He glanced down at where the baby was sleeping. "But tell me, Abby. What about Brianna's father? Didn't you kiss him like that?"

"Oh." She looked startled, as though she'd forgotten all about Brianna's father. Her face changed and she quickly turned it away. "I'm…uh…I don't really want to talk about that."

He shrugged, gaze darkening. There was quite a puzzle here and he was afraid it involved pain for Abby. He didn't want to make anything worse for her. But if she was in more trouble than she'd told him so far, he wanted to know what he could do to help her.

"Suit yourself," he said. "But when you're ready to talk about it, I'm ready to listen."

She met his gaze and he groaned. He could see by the look in her eyes that she'd come back down to earth and was remembering that she shouldn't be doing this. She was putting distance between them, even though she hadn't moved.

"Abby," he began, reaching out for her hand.

But she pulled it away and slid down off the bed. "We really ought to get some sleep," she said. "You've got to get well and I've got to…"

Her voice trailed off and she looked away. Her face averted, she closed her eyes and pressed her lips together, moaning internally. What had she done? Was she crazy? She knelt to check on Brianna, then rose and turned off the lantern without looking in his direction again.

"Good night," she murmured, and stumbled her way to the love seat.

"Abby," he said again, concern obvious in his voice. "You didn't do anything wrong. That whole thing was my fault." She didn't answer and he spoke again, more softly. "And I don't regret it. You are without a doubt the sweetest girl I've ever kissed."

Lying in the dark, she rolled her eyes. Sweet! Wonderful. That was not exactly what she wanted to be. Not when the prince so obviously preferred smart, experienced women like his cousin Nadia. If she didn't answer would he assume she was already asleep?

"Good night, Abby," he said. "See you in the morning."

She didn't respond and to her chagrin, tears began to spill from her eyes. She was in an impossible situation and now she'd done all she could to make things worse. She'd gone and let herself get a deep, stinging crush on the prince. *Way to go, numbskull!*

She wiped her eyes, being careful not to sniff too loudly. And then she let her senses go back over what had just happened here. His voice, his touch, his kiss. Gregor had warned her not to let herself get involved with the prince. Was this what he'd meant? Or was there more? Lying here in the dark, she longed to hold him, stroke his firm body, feel him take possession of hers. And yet she knew it could never happen. Never in a hundred years.

Abby was dreaming. Mychale had just kissed her again and she was floating just above her bed. Magic. She looked across the room and there was Mychale. "Stay," he said, reaching for her, the look on his handsome face one that would be hard to resist. Her heart seemed to swell in her chest. Then she looked to the other side of the room and there was Gregor. "Don't fall for the prince," he was warning, looking worried. She knew he was right.

"I won't," she murmured sleepily.

"Won't what?" Mychale whispered close to her ear.

"Fall in love," she muttered. "Oh!" She opened her eyes and then shot up into a sitting position. She wasn't asleep any longer and Mychale was really there, standing right beside the love seat. "What…?"

"It's okay," he reassured her, putting a hand on her shoulder. "It's just that Brianna's awake. I thought you might want to know."

"Oh. Yes." She blinked for a few seconds, then came fully awake herself and swung her legs off the love seat, rising and hurrying toward where the baby was whimpering in her bed.

Mychale watched as she lifted Brianna and cooed to her, rocking her in her arms. He'd turned on the lantern, but at its lowest setting and the muted light and colors made the room feel intimate.

"You should get back in bed," Abby said, looking at him over Brianna's downy head. His sleek dark hair was falling down over his forehead, shadowing his eyes and making them look dark and dangerous. He was wearing nothing but loose-fitting pajama bottoms and looking incredibly sexy, but she was determined not to let that affect her—or at any rate, not to let how much it did affect her show.

"How are you feeling?"

He shrugged. "Pretty much normal," he said. "I don't think you have to worry about me anymore."

She frowned. "It can come on you suddenly. We've seen that."

He nodded. "I still feel a little fragile. But not on the edge of the precipice. I'm going to be okay. Thanks to you."

She flushed and he grinned. He loved how candidly she reacted. He also loved how she looked in her filmy nightgown with her yellow hair spilling around her shoulders like liquid gold.

"You were talking in your sleep," he told her.

This time she blanched. "No!"

"Yes. It was pretty interesting."

She looked stricken, clutching Brianna to her chest. "You can't control the crazy things you dream about," she protested. "It didn't mean a thing."

He favored her with an arch smile. "Didn't it?"

"No."

His gaze caressed her face. "How do you know what it was?"

"I don't. But..." She glared at him. "Okay. Tell me. What did I say?"

He hesitated. Now that it came down to it, he rather wished he hadn't brought it up. Too late now.

"You said you wouldn't fall in love," he told her, watching her reaction with narrowed eyes. "You were quite adamant about it."

Now her cheeks were bright red. "Well, what's wrong with that?" she said stoutly, rubbing Brianna's back with a rhythmic motion.

He held back a chuckle. "Nothing's wrong with it. It's just interesting."

Drawing breath deep into her lungs, she turned to face him, looking severe. "You think you're getting some deep psychological insight into my dark subconscious?" she asked with just a hint of sarcasm. "I'll give you more. I am quite determined not to let myself fall in love. I've got to keep my mind clear and priorities straight. I've got a baby to raise. That's my focus. I can't let myself get lost in the woods."

He raised one dark eyebrow, looking amused. "Falling in love is like getting lost in the woods?"

"Absolutely. And running headfirst into a tree."

He laughed aloud. "Abby, you're one of a kind," he said, looking at her with so much affection, she had to turn away from his gaze.

But he quickly sobered and looked at her seriously. "Tell me this, Abby. Did you love Brianna's father?"

"No."

There was no hesitation in her response. That made him smile. And for some reason, it even made him happy. He wasn't sure why.

"Then who are you so determined not to fall in love with now?" he teased, pretty sure he knew the answer.

She paused, closed her eyes for a moment, as though she were counting to ten, then opened them and looked him straight in the eye. "You, of course. I'm very carefully guarding against it."

"I see." He supposed he shouldn't be surprised at her honesty any longer. You'd think he would be used to it by now. But it was still refreshing. He liked her. He really, really liked her.

"But it's okay," she was saying. "Don't worry about me. I'm leaving soon and I know you can't really fall in love in two or three days."

He frowned, searching her eyes. "Who says you can't?" he asked softly.

Her tongue made a quick pass over her lips, as though they were dry, but she spoke firmly. "I say so."

He shook his head. "What about love at first sight?"

"It's a myth. That's just infatuation."

He started to smile again, his eyelids heavy as he moved toward her. He might be teasing her but she couldn't know for sure and her heart was beginning to race in her chest. The atmosphere was too intimate, the air too full of possibilities. She was going to have to find a way to defuse the situation quickly.

"What's wrong with a little infatuation between friends?" he asked as he came closer, his tone just barely suggestive.

"Ah hah!" She pointed at him, backing away. "You stop right there. You promised you wouldn't try to seduce me. And you're going to keep that promise."

That concept seemed to stun him. "Why would I keep such a stupid promise?"

Again she didn't have to grope for an answer. "Because you're a Montenevada." Her chin rose as though she would show him the way. "Because you uphold the honor of your family name. Because you have character."

He stopped and stared at her. It had been a long time since anyone had used this angle with him. But it did sound familiar, with echoes of things his mother had said to him as a boy. He frowned, beginning to feel like she was winning this one. Character was one of those annoying attributes that kept you from having fun a lot of the time, but it looked like she was bound and determined to make sure that happened anyway.

"I do?"

"Yes." Her eyes flashed. "And if you don't think you've got it yet, you'd better start developing it. Because you have a country to run."

He winced as though she'd hit her mark, but not quite in the way she'd intended.

"That's where you're wrong," he said softly, his eyes darkening "My brothers run the country. I'm just genetic backup in case they don't have sons."

CHAPTER EIGHT

ONCE Brianna was awake, she didn't seem to see any point in going back to sleep again. Staying up was much more appealing. So she looked at the world with huge, bright eyes and began to fuss when she felt people weren't paying enough attention.

"That does it," Abby said at last. "Here, hold the baby." And she plopped the little one into the prince's arms.

"Wait a minute," he said, alarmed. "Wasn't this where I came in?"

"It's one of those reoccurring tasks we all have to tend to at one time or another," she told him sternly. "Be a man about it."

"I don't think a man is what this baby wants," he said, holding her gingerly.

Abby held back her smile. "I'll be back in a minute. I just need to warm her bottle a little."

"Right." Mychale looked down at the child squirming in his arms and sighed. "You're stuck with me, kid. Let's see if you like my pacing as much as you do your mom's."

Abby loved the picture they made, the two of them together, but she knew he was uncomfortable so she hurried through the bottle warming and got back as quickly as she could. Taking Brianna into her arms, she prepared to feed her. To her surprise, the baby pulled away and wouldn't take the bottle. That was unusual. With a weary shrug, she put her up against her shoulder again and began to walk the room.

Mychale was back leaning against the headboard and watching. Suddenly he groaned and she turned in surprise to look at him.

"Okay, Abby," he said looking reluctant to say it. "This is going to sound a little weird, but I swear she's reaching for me."

Smiling was one thing. But reaching? That was going a little too far. She was only an infant, for heaven's sake.

"Be serious," she scoffed.

"But she is." He shook his head, looking at her. "She reached out her little arm and kind of made a lunge toward me as you passed. I saw her."

"That's ridiculous."

He shrugged, a mere victim of circumstances beyond his control. "It might seem so on the surface. But you're forgetting." A glint of humor appeared in his gaze. "I have a powerful magnetism for females of all ages. Believe me, I know the look."

Oh brother! She had to bite her lip to keep from laughing. But she had to admit, the arm *had* flung out. She'd felt it go. But it didn't mean a thing. "It was an involuntary reflex," she explained. "It has nothing to do with you."

"Oh really?" His eyebrow rose. "Face it, Abby," he said, looking smug. "She likes me."

"Well, of course she likes you." She cupped the downy

top of Brianna's head lovingly. "Why not? To her you're just a big blob of friendly male on her tiny horizon."

He smiled. "You're jealous."

"That she likes you? I'm sure the countryside is littered with people who like you." She stopped before him, realizing she was sounding a little defensive. "Okay, mister. If you're so sure she is yearning for the fatherly touch, here. You take her. And take the bottle, too. Let's see if you can do better than I did."

She watched as the baby melted into his arms and accepted the bottle willingly. He looked up and gave a small shrug, as if to say, *you just never know, do you?*

She shook her head and laughed softly, then watched in wonder as his face took on a look of something close to rapture.

"Wow," he said softly. "Why does this feel so good?"

"Life," she said softly, feeling a glow as she watched. "Small, beginning life. It's magic and precious."

He nodded in agreement. "It's something primal, isn't it? You'd think that generations of being royal would have snuffed it out, but here it is."

She shook her head. "Why would being royal make a difference?"

He looked up at her. "Royalty tends to be unbelievably self-absorbed."

She held back the smile that threatened at his words. "Really?"

"Self-centered pigs," he muttered, stroking the little head.

She made a face. "That's a little harsh."

"But true."

"Oh, I don't know...." Her words faded away and she

laughed. "You're putting me in the position of defending royalty," she pointed out.

He gave her his patented lopsided grin. "Why not? You've lived around the margins of royalty all your life, haven't you? You know all about us."

"Hardly." But she thought of something and she sat down next to him on the bed.

"So what made you say that about your brothers?" she asked.

He didn't look up. "What did I say?"

She studied his chiseled profile. "You made it sound like you think you're irrelevant."

"Nonsense. I'm not really that prone to self-pity." Brianna had finished the bottle and was looking very close to sleep. He gently pulled the bottle from her mouth and handed it to Abby. "I am, however, something of a realist. And it's obvious, isn't it? They were both heroes of the war. I wasn't."

"You weren't here," she said as she took the baby from him. "You were in training in America and in England. I remember reading about it."

"Exactly."

She frowned at him. "You can't be blamed for that."

"It's not a matter of being blamed. It's a matter of fact. I didn't do much to help get us our country back, therefore I don't deserve to take my place with the heroes." His eyes darkened. "Look at your friend Gregor. He did more than I did and he lost his eyesight in one eye."

She settled Brianna in her bed, then rose and turned to look at him. Without knowing more about what exactly he did do during the war, she couldn't counter his own self-criticism. But she knew instinctively that he was wrong. Just knowing the man made her know that.

"Is that why you agreed to marry Stephanie?" she asked him. "Is that your way of doing your part?"

He stared at her for a long moment before he answered. "Very perceptive of you, Abby. Yes. Dane came to me and asked me to do it. I felt I had to, since it was past time for me to do something to help get this country established again."

Abby nodded, her heart aching. She'd seen pictures of the woman. You couldn't avoid them. The paparazzi loved her, and so did the society pages. She was very beautiful, but in pictures, her eyes always looked blank. Abby winced, thinking of those eerie eyes. "She's rich."

"Incredibly rich. And we need money. Plus, her father is very influential in international circles. He can help us in ways too numerous to count."

A pang of agony seemed to shiver through her. "Do you love her?"

He didn't answer but he didn't have to. The look on his face said it all.

"Mychale…" She went to him, looking up, her eyes wide and full of passion. "Don't do it. Please. Don't marry her."

He caught her with both hands, holding her face before him. He searched her eyes as though looking for something precious he might have lost there. "I promised I would."

"Break your promise," she urged. "Better a broken promise than two broken lives."

A humorless smile twisted his handsome face. "But what about that Montenevada character thing?" he asked her.

Her breath caught in her throat and she shook her head. He had her there. "Life is complex," she murmured. "Things aren't always so easy, are they?"

A slow smile began to fill his eyes and instead of answering her, he bent and touched her lips with his. One sweet, tender kiss, and that was all. But now Abby was sure of it. She was in love.

Brianna's wakefulness had taken them right from the midnight check period until just an hour short of the 3:00 a.m. designation when she finally drifted off.

"You might as well turn off the alarm," Mychale told Abby. "You need to get some sleep."

She sank onto the love seat and yawned. "What about you?"

"I've had plenty of rest in the last couple of days." Rising, he started for the door. "I think I'll go out and get some of that reading material Gregor left for me. I'm too wide-awake to go back to sleep just yet and it feels good to be able to walk around again."

"All right," she murmured groggily. "Leave the light on if you're going to read. It doesn't bother me at all."

She lay back and smiled to herself. What a strange night this had been. Strange, yet oddly wonderful. She wouldn't have missed it for the world.

She had almost sunk into sleep when Mychale came back into the room. Her eyes barely opened to register him until he paused beside the love seat, then bent down to drop a kiss on her face. She smiled at him. His casual affection for her was a revelation. She only wished it meant anything other than a sort of surface attraction.

"G'night," she whispered.

As he straightened and turned toward the bed, she heard a paper sound. Opening her eyes, she noticed that a small tabloid-size newspaper had slipped out from between the magazines he was carrying. It fluttered to the floor. She opened her eyes more widely and stared at the headline lying a few feet away.

"No Leads In Search For Missing Baby."

Her heart stopped in her chest. Looking up, she could see that Mychale hadn't noticed the paper slip from his stack. He was making himself comfortable on the bed and looking through the magazines. As she watched, unable to breathe, he picked one and flipped it open, setting the others aside. Lying very still she waited and watched as he began to read.

What was she going to do? She had to get rid of this paper. Somehow, she had to hide it right in front of him. Her mouth was dry as she forced herself to breathe evenly. If she could just reach out without him seeing, she could grab the paper and stuff it under the cushion of the love seat. But how was she going to do it without him noticing? He would notice movement like that. He would hear the paper rustle if nothing else.

"What's the matter?" he asked suddenly, and she almost jumped out of her skin.

"Oh!" She gasped. "Uh, nothing. I just remembered I didn't turn the alarm off." She pulled herself up, swung her legs around and began to slip off the love seat.

"I'll do it," he said.

"No," she countered quickly. "Look, I'm already up. You just stay where you are and read."

He gave her a fleeting smile and did as she suggested. She breathed a sigh of relief. As she passed the paper, she used her bare foot to push it toward the dresser which stood against the wall. She turned off the alarm, her heart beating so loudly she was sure he must hear it, then turned back toward her makeshift bed. Just two more shoves with her foot should get the paper where Mychale couldn't see it from his position. That might keep her safe until morning when she could get up early and dispose of it without him seeing her. She kicked the paper further toward the dresser with one foot, then set the other to put in the final shove. She was almost home free when the prince looked up and noticed.

"Is that the newspaper I brought in with the magazines?" he asked. "I guess I must have dropped it."

She stopped, mid-kick, and tried to smile. "I guess so," she said weakly. "I'll just put it here on the dresser."

"Okay, fine. I can pick it from there if I get to it," he said.

She set the paper down, headlines hidden, and slunk on to the love seat, feeling like a liar and a thief. Whatever happened in the morning, she was going to have to deal with the paper. She only hoped she would be able to do it before he saw that headline. Because she was sure that once he saw it, there would be no stopping him from finding out the truth.

She had Brianna back in the maid's room and every sign she'd ever been with them wiped away from the main part of the house by the time Gregor showed up early the next morning. And she'd dealt with the newspaper. But she wasn't proud of what she'd done.

She went to the kitchen and fixed breakfast for both of them, using her last two eggs. And all the while her mind was on the newspaper still sitting on the dresser. But every time she thought she had a moment to duck back and destroy it, Mychale wanted her opinion on something or wanted her to see some new growth in the garden or to help him ooh and aah over Brianna blowing bubbles from her tiny baby lips. Finally she put half an omelet before him and slipped away. Grabbing the newspaper, she hurried back to the butler's pantry with it.

"Abby," the prince called. "While you're in there, could you pick up that newspaper? I might as well see what's going on in the world."

She froze. Now what?

"Okay," she called back, but she didn't move. What could she do? She couldn't let him read it. But she couldn't just tell him she'd ripped it up and thrown it away.

She gazed around the kitchen, desperately looking for a good idea. Then she picked up the coffee urn and stared at it. Dropping the newspaper into the sink, she poured hot coffee all over it.

"Oops," she whispered to herself, then closed her eyes and added, "Please forgive me, Mychale. If you can."

Walking out into the breakfast room, she managed a painful smile. "I'm so sorry, your highness, but I had a little accident. I spilled coffee all over the newspaper. I'm afraid it's ruined."

He looked up. "Are you calling me that because you

think I'm going to be angry?" he asked, incredulous. "Never mind." He smiled. "Just looking at you is better than reading anyway."

Guilt stabbed her like a knife. She tried to smile back but it was tough. He looked so handsome sitting there, the morning sun slanting in to warm his tan. Now that he was healthy again she could picture him on the deck of the yacht, cruising with the wind in his hair and the sun on his face. He looked downright royal—but more than that, strong and honorable, a man of distinction and class. She felt humbled. Filled with remorse, the urge to just tell him the truth and get it all out in the open came over her in a rush. Wouldn't that be better than this constant lying?

But before she could even hint at the things he ought to know about her, a car started up the driveway and they both turned to the window to see who it was.

"Gregor," Mychale said. "Good. I want him to assure you that I'm fine and you don't have to hover over me any longer." His smile took the sting out of his words. "Because I'm pretty sure it's true."

It was true. She knew that even before Gregor finished examining the prince and proclaimed it. So she was free. It was time to go.

But Gregor wouldn't leave. She fidgeted while he grumbled about the gate at the bottom of the driveway which needed repairing, then he and Mychale talked about various local issues. Abby was surprised at how much Mychale seemed to know about the area problems, and how much he seemed to care. Finally they wrapped it up and Gregor hurried off to go down to the hospital to consult on the two burned hatchery workers, saying he would stop by again in the evening. Abby turned to look at Mychale and realized just how much she was going to miss him.

It was on the tip of her tongue to tell him she was going to go prepare Brianna for the trip. After all, that was what he'd originally wanted. But looking at him, she suddenly knew that was going to be impossible. He didn't want her to leave any longer. He didn't want Brianna to leave. He was going to resist, and she was going to have to sneak away.

Her heart sank. She was so tired of the subterfuge. Was she going to be living the rest of her life this way?

She went to the kitchen to clean up from breakfast and Mychale came along, reading to her from one of the magazines Gregor had brought. It was an article about the wonders of the lake country flora and fauna, and he began planning to take her and Brianna on a picnic to his favorite local haunt. She was only half listening. She had to make her own plans. There would be no picnic for her and her baby.

At least she'd decided exactly where they would go. The small city of Dharma, where the royal family had set up their winter palace in exile, was within reach. It was an area she knew fairly well, having lived there for parts of the last three or four winters. She would be careful to stay away from the sections where she was likely to be recognized.

But her old French tutor lived in the bohemian part of town. He and his wife had been special friends, until her uncle had begun stiffing him on his tutoring bills and there had been a falling out between them. Maybe they would take her in until she could get her feet on the ground. They might enjoy a bit of revenge against her uncle. It was worth a try.

"You aren't listening to me." Mychale had come up behind her and now his arms slid around her, pulling her in close to his hard body.

"I'm going to have to resort to the touch system," he murmured. He buried his face in her hair and then he began a trail of kisses down the side of her neck. She closed her eyes, reveling in pure sensation.

His hands cupped her breasts and she arched into his caress. Would it be so wrong to make love with this man? It would be crazy. But desire for him was burning its way through her body. Everywhere he touched was sizzling.

She turned, raising her arms to give him access to every part of her, sinking her fingers into his thick hair, moaning low and deep in her throat. She was already his emotionally. Why not make it physical as well?

He was muttering something against her skin but there was a buzzing in her ears and she couldn't make out the words. She wanted him, wanted this. She was about to leave and sure to spend the rest of her life on the run. Could she allow herself this one bit of happiness?

"Hello! Anybody home?"

Abby clung to Mychale for as long as it took to process the fact that someone new was in the house. And then she pulled back quickly, dread growing in her heart. She had waited too long. Why oh why hadn't she left when she had the chance?

He touched her cheek and looked down at her with such affection, it almost made up for everything. "Abby, we aren't done here. Just remember…"

She kissed his hand and then the two of them swung

around just in time to see the prince's cousin Nadia stride gracefully around the corner and into the room. She was tall and thin as a runway model and dressed just as flamboyantly in modish black and purple. Her jet-black hair was pulled into a sleek chignon and accented by huge dark sunglasses which she had planted atop her head. Her face was pretty but careful, as though she were posing for pictures.

"Hello there," she said, putting out a cheek for Mychale to kiss but looking at Abby, whose mouth went dry as she looked for evidence that Nadia recognized her. "I thought I'd find you here. I have to warn you, I raced on ahead of the others, but they are on their way. They're probably an hour or so behind me."

Mychale groaned. "Oh, no. Is there any way we can head them off?"

She shrugged extravagantly. "Flares and border guards with missile launchers perhaps. Anything else is doomed to failure."

Mychale's brow lowered darkly. "How did you know I was here?" he said suspiciously. "Did Gregor Narna have anything to do with this?"

"Gregor Narna?" Nadia looked at him blankly. "No, it was your friend Andrew. He remembered visiting here as a teenager. Once he said it, I knew this had to be where you'd gone." Her smile was sunny. "It's the usual bunch and they feel you've neglected them for days and days. They're loaded for bear and not going to take no for an answer."

"They may have to find someone else to hang with in the future," Mychale groused. "This constant moving party is getting old."

"Ouch. Defectors are not regarded kindly in our crowd," she reminded him gently. "Better keep that in mind." She turned her beautiful dark eyes on his companion. "But I see you wanted a little privacy. I hope I'm not interrupting anything crucial."

"Nadia, this is Abby. I'm falling in love with her so treat her kindly."

Abby flushed but it was obvious he was merely making an outrageous claim in the spirit of the surface chatter Nadine and his regular group of friends dealt in. Nadine didn't seem to take it any more seriously than she did. And even more important, she didn't seem to have a clue as to who Abby was. Extending a hand, she gave her a brief smile, then turned her attention back on her cousin.

"Tell me, my dear, have you gotten over your recent shipboard snit?" she asked him. "Are you ready to welcome your betrothed back into your embrace? Will you clutch her to your bosom?"

He grimaced, raking a hand through his hair. "Hell no. I don't ever want to see that woman again. And I'm prepared to tell Dane as much when I get back to the palace."

Nadine pursed her lips. "He'll work on your guilt," she reminded him. "He'll threaten to disown you."

"That's the least of my worries," he said cavalierly, pacing the floor in front of them. "Let him disown me. I don't need royal status. In fact," he added, looking at Abby with a gleam in his eye, "it might just make life easier without it."

"So, that's truly the way the land lies," Nadine said wisely, giving Abby a tight smile. "Then I guess it's just as well I put an end to your engagement myself."

He swung around and stared at her. "What?"

She pulled a ring and a piece of paper out of her handbag. "I have here one engagement ring and a signed release stating that Miss Stephanie Hollenbeck has severed all matrimonial ties with you for the foreseeable future."

He grabbed the paper and studied it critically, then turned his gaze on his cousin. "How the hell did you get her to sign this thing?" he asked, still skeptical.

Nadine waved a hand in the air. "I have my ways. The ring was a bigger problem. She was going to keep it. I'm sure she was planning to hock it herself. So I ripped it off her finger."

Mychale laughed aloud. "You didn't."

"I did. She was saying she wasn't going to marry you because you had treated her so abominably, that you were going to have to come crawling back on your hands and knees to beg her forgiveness if you wanted her hand—and her family money."

"That'll be the day."

"I told her if she had any pride at all she would break the engagement off totally and not leave you an option of return. She thought it over—well, she tried. Her thinking ability leaves something to be desired. But she realized I was right. So she did as I suggested. And I have it here in writing." She made a flourish with her hand. "Problem solved. Cousin Nadia to the rescue, as usual."

Mychale looked at Abby. "Didn't I tell you she was fantastic? Get friendly with her. She'll do things for you, too."

"But of course." Nadia's smile actually seemed real to Abby for the first time and she smiled back.

"Now I just have to tell Dane about it," Mychale said, looking less than optimistic.

"You're on your own with that one," Nadia said. "He terrifies me."

"He terrifies everyone," Mychale agreed, nodding. "But he's going to be the ruler of our country, not our private lives. It's time I make sure we have an understanding on that score."

"Yes," Nadia agreed. "But wait until I'm out of town, would you? I don't relish being hit by the cross fire."

Mychale gave her a look. "I imagine you're planning to stay here tonight. Do you have bags?"

"In the car. No serving staff?"

"Just me, your humble porter," he said with a cynical gleam. "I'll get them. I want to take a look at the gate at the bottom of the driveway anyway. The latch isn't working." He waved a hand. "You two talk among yourselves."

Abby watched him head for the door with fear making a lump in her throat. She had to get out of here before the others arrived. She only wished she'd made her getaway before Nadia had appeared, but it was too late to remedy that now.

Nadia was staring at her with a bemused look on her sophisticatedly beautiful face. "How did you do it?" she asked.

Abby's heart jumped, then quieted again when she realized Nadia wasn't talking about a kidnapping charge. "Do what?"

"Make him fall in love with you."

Her mouth dropped open in surprise. "But I didn't!"

"Of course you did. I've seen him infatuated before, but I've never seen him look at a woman the way he looks at you. Congratulations, my dear. Now the next thing is…" Her dark eyes narrowed. "Don't break his heart or I'll have to scratch your eyes out."

Break the prince's heart? What was the woman talking about?

"I don't think there's much chance of that," she responded with a half-laugh. "I…I'm leaving soon and…"

But Nadia was frowning as she looked her over. "Wait a minute. Don't I know you?"

CHAPTER NINE

ABBY'S heart sank. She should have known this was coming. "I'm not sure...."

"What is your full name?" Nadia asked, studying her face.

Here it was. She couldn't fudge this one. Her mind raced trying to think of a way out, but there was none. Nadia had asked a simple question. She deserved a simple answer.

"Abby Donair."

"I do know you," she said. "You're the doctor's niece, aren't you?" She looked completely baffled. "What are you doing here? Everyone is looking for you."

Pure panic shivered through her but she knew she couldn't show it and she kept her face bland. "Really?"

"Yes." Nadia's gaze narrowed as she looked her over. "They say you took the baby."

"The baby?" She suddenly noticed one of Brianna's bibs was peeking out from under a throw pillow at the corner of the couch. Her gaze was riveted to it as she squeaked out, "What baby?"

But Nadia's mind was on the puzzle, not her

response. Abby took the opportunity to move toward the couch, trying to look casual.

"Yes," Nadia said, frowning, her forefinger to her chin. "But here you are with Mychale. So I guess that was a red herring. Hmm."

Abby reached down and pushed the bib further under the pillow. Looking up, she didn't think Nadia had caught that bit of business and she breathed a sigh of relief. The tall, beautiful woman was so busy trying to figure out what was going on in the palace mystery, she didn't notice clues right in front of her. Abby felt lucky, at least for the moment.

"Everyone is running around with his hair on fire and here you are, hiding out with Mychale in the country, cool as you please." Her face scrunched with suspicion for just a moment. "Is there something going on? I didn't even know that you two knew each other."

Abby smiled and looked away. There was no point in trying to explain. Anything like that would only draw her deeper and deeper into trouble.

Nadia didn't seem to mind the lack of an answer. She sank down onto the couch, leaning against the pillow that was hiding the bib and patting the cushion beside her, inviting Abby to sit down for a chat.

"We've never gotten to know each other, you and I, but I have heard about you and of course, I've seen you at various palace functions. Teas and luncheons, I think. No?"

Abby nodded, taking a seat beside her and surprised to find that she liked the woman a lot more than she'd expected to, despite everything.

"Well, I've always liked what I saw of you and your

sister—my condolences, by the way. Such a terrible thing." She shook her head and took Abby's hand in hers for a moment. "I know you must be devastated."

Abby nodded silently, blinking back sudden tears.

Nadia smiled her sympathy, then frowned again. "But I have to say, I don't know if I trust that uncle of yours. Do you know what he's doing?"

Abby shrugged. "I haven't talked to him for days," she said truthfully. Actually she wanted to hear how he'd presented his case to the world. She'd known he was going to claim Julienne's baby was royal, but she hadn't been there to witness just how he went about it. "And we've been pretty much incommunicado up here lately. So I really have no idea."

Nadia frowned. "Well, he's got this story about a baby sired by Crown Prince Dane when he was wounded and out of his mind for that awful month at the end of the war. But as far as I'm concerned, it doesn't really hold together. There seems to be something fishy going on there." She looked at Abby sideways. "Was there ever a baby? No one seems to have seen it."

"Yes, well…" Abby averted her gaze. That stubborn sense of panic was back. What on earth could she say to this woman? "When I get home I'll…uh…I'll see if I can get to the bottom of things."

Nadia seemed to accept that as an admission that the baby's existence might be a hoax. "Good. And listen, call on me if you need any help. Don't feel you have to stay with your uncle if it's not a good situation. I have resources."

Oh, if only she could do that. Nadia was just the sort

of person she would love to have covering her back. Unfortunately, once Nadia knew all, she wasn't going to feel much like defending Abby. Of that, she was sure.

In the meantime, she had to go. The need to leave was so urgent, she was on pins and needles. How was she going to get away from Nadia and Mychale so that she could grab Brianna and get out of here?

"Uh, listen, you must be tired from your drive. Would you like to…?"

"What I'd like would be a drink of water," Nadia interjected, pretending to clutch at her throat.

"Great. Come on into the kitchen." Abby led the way and poured water into a glass, which Nadia accepted gratefully.

"I'm so glad you've come to keep him company," she told the cousin as they walked back into the breakfast room. She was thinking this might be a good time to begin to withdraw and prepare to flee. "Because I'm going to have to…uh…get going. I've got obligations to take care of."

"No problem," Nadia told her warmly. "Mychale and I are best friends and have been since we were kids. I'll stay as long as he needs me."

Abby nodded gratefully. Looking out the front window, she saw that Mychale was fixing the broken gate at the bottom of the driveway. She still had a moment or two, and there were a few things she really ought to say. Impulsively she turned to Nadia.

"I think you should know that he's been very sick."

Nadia's eyes widened. "What?"

"Yes. He's had that disease that attacks the balance that supposedly runs in the family."

Nadia shook her head, looking worried. "I don't know anything about that. Has a doctor seen him?"

"Yes. A local man. He was very bad for a while. I was really frightened." She shivered, remembering. "But he's better now. And since you're here, you'll be able to take care of him."

"Oh, of course. I'm so glad you were here to help him." She put a hand over her heart. "At first I thought you were going to tell me he'd been in a deep depression. I keep expecting it, the way he beats himself up over…Well, I'm sure you know."

"No." Abby looked at her curiously. "What do you mean?"

Nadia waved a hand in the air. "Oh, it's just the war thing. Never mind." She folded her arms in front of her and restlessly paced a few steps, then turned back to Abby. "No matter what you say, I'll bet it had something to do with him being ill like that. It might have set the stage, who knows?"

Abby shook her head, completely at sea. "I don't know what you're talking about," she admitted.

"Oh. The war, of course." Nadia looked disconcerted, then suddenly resolute. "Well, that's it. I'm going to do it. I promised him I wouldn't, but enough is enough." She looked intense and highly emotional. "He deserves some recognition. Don't you think? And I'm going to make sure he gets some."

"Nadia," Abby said, catching hold of her by the hands. "What are you talking about?"

The woman stared right into her eyes. "I'm going to go to Dane. He scares me to death, but I'm going to do it. I've been thinking about it for so long and I just haven't had the nerve. But that's over. I'm going to do it."

Abby squeezed her hands in frustration. "Do what?"

Nadia's chin rose. "Convince Dane that Mychale deserves a commendation for bravery. There's no one else to plead his case. He certainly won't do it for himself."

Abby shook her head. "What did he do?"

"A lot of things. Things that never got any recognition." She sighed, still holding Abby's hands in hers. "You know how it was there at the end of the war. Everything seemed to explode at once, like a fireworks factory blew up or something. Dane and Nico were both big heroes and everyone knows all the good, brave things they did to win back their country. But Mychale was the youngest brother. They sent him overseas to school and for training and by the time he got back the war was almost over. He didn't have much time to do heroic things."

"Oh. Yes, actually, he did say something about that." Abby's heart cracked a little, just thinking about the situation Mychale must have found himself in. To have two older brothers considered such heroes by one and all… She remembered some of the things he'd said. Hadn't he hinted at this very thing during the night when he'd talked about what Gregor had sacrificed and that he hadn't done enough himself?

"But he did so many things anyway," Nadia was continuing. "And he saved an entire village. He singlehandedly rooted out the enemy and killed two of them who were trying to burn down the village. He saved the mayor and his family from certain death." She threw up her hands. "But he did all this just two days before the victory. When he got back and the story began to be told, it was drowned out by the explosion of joy over the liberation. His brothers don't even know."

"That's just not right," Abby said, ready to join Nadia's crusade.

"No. He made me swear to be quiet about it. He didn't want any fuss." Nadia shook her head. "But I've had it. I'm going to tell them and make them do something to acknowledge it."

"I think you should. Definitely." Her heart seemed to swell as she thought of how he'd been left behind by current history. Something should be done before it was lost and too late. "He deserves it."

"You better believe it." Nadia's eyes flashed. "And more than that, he needs it. I know it eats away at him all the time."

They still clasped hands and stared into each other's eyes, united in their emotion. Love for Mychale, Abby realized, was what had brought them together.

But their moment of sisterhood lasted only seconds. A car horn sounded, and then another, and Nadia dropped Abby's hands as she turned to look out the front window.

"Oh drat, they're already here. Are you ready for a nonstop party?"

"Not at all," Abby said fervently. "In fact, I think I'll go take a nap and rest up for the trip I'm going to have to take."

Nadia gave her a pat on the shoulder. "You do that. I'll tell Mychale."

"Thanks."

She retreated with wings on her feet, hurrying to the maid's room where Brianna was just stirring. She began throwing things into a bag. She had to get out of here fast. She wouldn't dare take the bus now. It was too late for that. She would have to hike through the woods until she got to the border, carrying Brianna all the way. Well, so be it. She would do what she had to do. She'd stayed too long and now she would have to pay the price.

They would come after her, of course. But she'd bought some time in pretending to be taking a nap. Once they knew she was actually gone, Mychale would think she'd run to Gregor. And since the doctor was on his way to the hospital and wouldn't be back for hours, they would waste time in that direction and then search the village and the buses and trains before heading for her actual escape route. Just as long as they didn't tumble to the fact that she'd headed out of the country, she would gain some time. All that might just delay them long enough for her to get over the border. If only she could have a little luck.

Ten minutes later she was out the back door and starting for the woods. She only let herself look back once, when she came to the first trees and could partly stand behind one. She looked at the big old beautiful house with its dark wood, the glass panes reflecting the sun, the driveway, now full of cars.

And there, for just a moment, was Mychale. He'd come out to see someone's car, a fancy new roadster. He looked so tall and elegant with his dark hair falling over his forehead. The group around him was laughing and joking, and so was he. They were obviously good friends and he fit right in. And she never would.

Not that her fitting in with the royal set was here nor there. What did it matter? She would probably never see him again.

Her heart lurched at the thought. She was in love with a man she could never, ever have. Would it have been better not to love at all? No. She wouldn't have traded away the last few days for anything in the world. A broken heart was better than nothing, and before she'd met the prince, she'd had nothing.

"Nothing but a baby to love forever," she whispered, hugging Brianna close. "And that'll do me from now on."

Turning resolutely, she began the long trudge through the woods.

Prince Mychale enjoyed seeing his friends again—for about half an hour. And then he began to wonder how long Abby's nap was going to last. He was tempted to peek in and see if Brianna was awake. He was looking forward to showing her to Nadia—and showing off his new baby-friendly ways. But he decided to let them both sleep.

Another hour went by. The happy-go-lucky jocularity of his friends was beginning to wear thin. Did these people really have nothing better to do with their lives than to sit around drinking wine and playing the occasional game or listening to music? The jokes were old. He'd heard them all before. He began to long for Abby.

Another half hour and he couldn't take it any longer. He knew the baby had to be kept quiet, but surely Abby could come out and meet everyone.

On the other hand, he might just be of a mind to keep her to himself.

"Where are you going?" Nadia asked, as bored with the others as he was. She'd been out walking around the property with another young woman, but now they were back and Nadia was looking for something interesting to do.

"I'm going to see how Abby is," he told her. "Want to come along?"

"Why not? It's always entertaining to watch love in bloom."

To her surprise, he didn't deny it. "Always glad to please," he said with a grin. "Come along. I've got a surprise to show you."

He led her down the back hall to the maid's room.

"Why did you salt her away back here?" Nadia grumbled. "You have all those beautiful bedrooms upstairs."

"There's a reason," he said. "You'll see."

He knocked on the door. "Abby? Are you awake?"

There was no answer and he knew right away that the silence was deeper and more foreboding than he would have expected.

"Abby?" He turned the knob, opening the door onto the empty room. Even the drawer that had been Brianna's bed was put back in its dresser.

He stared for a moment, stunned. He hadn't expected this at all. If anything, the feelings that had been growing between them should have precluded it. How could she leave without saying anything to him? It took him a moment to actually believe she'd done just that.

He turned to Nadia, bewildered. "She's gone. And she took the baby."

Nadia's dark eyebrows rose. "What baby?"

He shook his head, trying to clear his mind. "Her baby. She had her baby with her."

Nadia grabbed his wrist with her long fingers. "Wait

a minute, Mychale," she said firmly. "Abby Donair does not have a baby. I don't believe she's ever even been pregnant."

He looked at her as though she were nuts. "She has a baby. A baby named Brianna. I've held her myself."

Nadia gasped. "That must have been her sister Julienne's baby."

"What are you talking about?" he demanded, completely at sea.

Nadia sighed, looking at him sadly as her shoulders sagged. "Don't you see? She stole her sister's baby. Haven't you heard about it? Hasn't anyone told you?"

He shook his head. A feeling of dread filled his heart. Nadia knew things he didn't and somehow it was all making sense. The pieces were beginning to fall into place.

"Tell me," he said simply.

Nadia cringed. "Oh, Mychale, I wish I didn't have to."

"Talk."

She took a deep breath. "You know all those rumors about Dane having fathered a baby during that black period just before the restoration, when he was wounded and missing and so out of it he can't remember what he did?"

"Yes. Go on."

"Well, it seems that just a few days ago, Dr. Zaire came out and said his niece, Julienne had died giving birth and that the baby was Dane's. He says the DNA is a match. He presented the evidence to Dane himself. And as he's the expert on these things, everyone has been in a tizzy ever since."

"Dr. Zaire said that?" Mychale frowned, trying to tie that in with things Abby had told him. But when you came right down to it, it didn't work. The whole thing just didn't make sense.

"Yes. He had to make it public because the baby was missing and it was theorized that Julienne's sister, Abby, had run off with it. The secret service has been combing the country." She shook her head in consternation. "I asked her about it, first thing, and she didn't seem to know a thing about it. And she was so nice and you were so obviously smitten, that I just assumed the whole thing was a crazy story…" Her voice trailed off and she clutched his arm.

"Oh, Mychale. She's run off with Dane's baby."

"So you're back." Crown Prince Dane stared across his desk at his youngest sibling. Though just as handsome as his brothers, he was a few inches shorter and a whole lot tougher looking. He had the air of a man who'd been in a fight or two—and won.

"Yes, I'm back." Prince Mychale slumped down into a chair and looked levelly at his brother.

"Where exactly have you been?"

"I've been up at the château in the lake country. I needed some time alone. I've been thinking about my life and my place in the scheme of things. The *royal* scheme of things."

Dane grunted his distaste. "Too much thinking of that sort will turn you soft. Better to get an honest day's work done than to spend all that time thinking."

Mychale threw back his head and tried to smile. Same old Dane. He never changed.

"Now what's this nonsense about you breaking your engagement to the Hollenbeck girl?" he barked out.

Mychale looked him squarely in the eye. "It's true. It seemed like a good plan when it was on paper. In reality, it didn't work. The woman is a harridan. I won't have her raising my children."

Dane frowned. "That's too bad. I thought she would be right down your alley. Isn't she a part of that jet-set crowd you seem to run with?"

Mychale winced. He supposed he deserved that. There was really no defense, was there?

Dane was glaring at him. "You know that her father is threatening to sue despite the release you got from her."

"Let him."

Dane looked astonished. "And who is going to pay if the judgment goes against us? You?"

Mychale gazed back with a steely look in his eyes. "If I have to. I don't care, Dane. I'm sorry if this ruins your plans but I'm not marrying her."

Dane stared at him with cold eyes for a long, long moment, but to Mychale's surprise, he didn't shout, didn't insist that Mychale give in. "Do you have some other woman in mind?" he asked at last.

Mychale took a deep breath. "That's not the point."

"Then it's true."

Mychale winced. He might have someone else in mind, but that someone was turning out to be an impossible match. He didn't know why he even cared any longer, but he did.

"That doesn't matter," he said. "But there is one thing I have to know. The baby that Dr. Zaire claims is a DNA match to you. Is it really your baby?"

Dane hesitated long enough to speak volumes. "Dr. Zaire says so."

Mychale's gaze sharpened. "But you don't remember…?"

"No. I don't remember a thing." He shrugged wearily. "It supposedly happened during that month when I was out of my mind. Dr. Zaire nursed me back to health, as you remember. He says that his niece and I were intimate during that period." He shrugged again. "What can I say? I don't remember a thing. And since she's gone…"

Mychale closed his eyes for a moment. "I see."

"The poor girl died in childbirth. I don't quite understand how that could have happened in this day and age. Health care is going to be a big issue with us once we get our feet under us. And now her sister has run off with the baby."

Mychale nodded, picturing Abby carrying Brianna, just as he'd seen her a few days ago. His heart ached to see them both again. What he wanted was some explanation, something he could accept. That, and Abby in his arms. But after all that had happened, he was afraid that might never come to pass.

"We have people searching the neighboring countries, Italy, Switzerland, even the Balkans. We're going to find that baby." Dane's voice hardened and he sounded more like his old self. "And when we do, Miss Abby Donair will be sorry she decided to become a kidnapper."

Mychale stared at his brother. There was no point in telling him about Abby, in explaining how she'd been with him at the château. It was evident no one had told him and it was probably best to leave it that way.

Mychale had spent the last two days searching and had come up with nothing. Right after he and Nadia had discovered the two of them missing, he'd raced to the local transportation stations, then to find Gregor, then to hunt in every nook and cranny he could think of, mar-shalling the help of Gregor and everyone else he could round up. He'd been so sure they would find her. And when it was finally obvious that wasn't going to happen right away, he'd been sick at heart.

He had to find her. She would have to pay for what she'd done. And that pretty much made it impossible to think they could ever be close again. But he had to know why she'd done it. He had to hear what she would have to offer by way of explanation. He wasn't going to be able to rest until he had his answers.

But there wasn't much point in trying to work through Dane to find Abby, either. It was quite obvious that anger and confusion was clouding his brother's mind. He was going to have to go directly to the secret service and get special access on his own. That was the only way he was going to know when they found Abby and Brianna. Just what he was going to do with that knowledge he wasn't sure. But he had to be there when they found her. He had to be the lead investigator at the scene. The agents would give him some time with her before they moved in if he played things right. He had to know the truth.

"By the way," Dane said suddenly. "I've been going over your request to be named governor of the northern provinces, including the lake country. Where did this sudden interest in provincial management come from?"

Mychale leashed his natural reaction to his brother's goading. "It may have slipped your mind but I have a man-agement degree, with graduate studies in economics."

"Book learning," Dane scoffed. "What have you ever actually managed?"

Mychale resisted the impulse to anger. That wouldn't

get him anywhere. And Dane was probably baiting him anyway. The only way to win with this autocratic brother of his was to show no fear and keep your sense of humor.

"I'll be managing the northern provinces once you get around to signing the decree," he said lightly. "Then you'll have many opportunities to second-guess every decision I make."

Dane stared at him with hard eyes, but there seemed to be the slightest twitch at the corners of his wide mouth.

"We've neglected the lake country for too long," Mychale went on. "It's going to take a lot of work to get it back up to speed. Unemployment is the worst in the country. The area needs a complete economic rival. They don't even have a fully qualified doctor in Larona. Something's got to be done."

"And you're the man to do it?"

"We'll see, won't we?"

Dane smiled. "Yes, we will. Actually I'm glad you're taking this step. I was wondering when you were going to admit you were part of this administration."

Mychale shrugged. "I'm in."

"Good. I'll have the papers signed by the end of the week."

Mychale nodded. He'd never really had any doubt about it, still it was a relief to have it settled. He rose to go.

"Sorry, Dane," he said. "Sorry about the Stephanie Hollenbeck thing." He hesitated, then added, "I'm sure they'll find the baby soon."

"Damn right they will," Dane muttered, turning his attention back to his work.

Mychale left the office, closing the door behind him.

His mood was dark, but it lightened when he spotted Nadia coming his way.

"Hey, beautiful," he said, smiling at her. She was looking exceptionally dolled up for this time of the afternoon.

"Hey, back," she replied.

"Where are you off to?" he asked, hoping to get a little company to help dispel this funk he was in.

"I'm hopping a flight to London in a bit. Jonas Trick's invited me to be his guest at the premiere of his new film. Want to come along?"

He shook his head. "No. I think my globe-trotting party days are over. I'm moving on."

"Growing up?" she guessed, looking almost sad as she patted his cheek.

"About time, don't you think?"

She nodded, looking at him lovingly, then glanced at her watch. "Gotta go," she said. "I'm meeting with Dane before I catch a ride to the airport."

"With Dane?" His eyebrows rose. "Is this a command performance?"

"Not at all. I asked to see him. I have something I want to tell him about."

He frowned. This wasn't like Nadia. "I don't get it. You usually avoid him like the plague."

She gave him a one-shouldered shrug and walked on by. "Maybe I'm growing up a little, too," she called back at him, just before knocking on Dane's office door. "See you later," she added with a wink. "And Mychale, I hope you find Abby soon. And get to the bottom of all this nonsense."

He nodded, turning away. He would find her. He had

to. He needed to hear the truth from her own lips. Funny, but despite everything, he knew that he would believe her. That didn't mean he would forgive her. But once he knew exactly what she'd done and why—then maybe he could go on with his life.

CHAPTER TEN

ABBY climbed the rickety stairs to the third floor room where she was staying, carrying two bags of groceries. Monsieur St. Jean, her old French tutor, had found the room for her and she'd been there for almost two weeks. Two more days and the transportation her tutor had arranged would be taking her—and Brianna—to Denmark.

"They won't find you so far away," he'd assured her. "You'll be able to start a new life in a wonderful country."

A country where she didn't know the language and had no friends, no work, no place to stay. But she hardly worried about that. She was moving in a fog of misery, just putting one foot in front of the other, getting through the day. At some point she would have to start planning for their future. For now, she was just surviving.

"Things will be better once we get to Denmark."

That was what she kept telling herself.

Balancing the grocery bags, she fumbled for the key and unlocked the door, then stepped into the dark apartment and shut it behind her. She put the bags down while she reached for the light switch. Light flooded the room, and there was Prince Mychale, sitting in the over-stuffed easy chair, facing her.

Her scream was more of a shrill gasp and she turned as though she was going to make a run for it. He was up and out of the chair and between her and the door before she could even take in a full breath.

"You don't seriously think you could get away with that again, do you?" he demanded.

She stared up at him. Despite everything, she was hungry for the sight of his handsome face and her gaze quickly ranged over every feature.

"How are you feeling?" she asked before she thought. "Are you completely over…?"

He grasped her shoulders and swore angrily. "Damn it, Abby. Why did you lie to me? Why did you steal Dane's baby? Why didn't you tell me?"

The words choked in his throat as her eyes filled with tears and he groaned, pulling her close as though compelled by a force he couldn't resist.

"Abby, Abby," he muttered, kissing her upturned face. "Why?"

"Oh, Mychale," she whispered, just as weak in the face of her emotions as he was to his, "I love you so much."

He kissed her hard, reacting to his own vulnerability as much as to her words. His heart was filled with anger and regret, and at the same time, his feelings for this woman couldn't be denied. She kissed him back, a gesture so full of love and surrender, it took his breath away. If only he could gather her up and carry her off to a desert island where they could fall in love and never have to face the rest of the world. He would do it in a heartbeat—if only it were possible.

"Abby, why? Why did you lie to me? Why did you run off with the baby?"

Abby sobbed and took a wavering breath. "I hated lying to you most of all. I tried not to. I mostly just didn't tell you things I should have told you. But I tried very hard to keep the actual lying to a minimum."

He shook his head, his eyes full of regret. "If you had only told me the truth, maybe we could have…"

"No." She put a hand up and touched his lips to stop him. "I couldn't tell you. You would have stopped me."

He gazed down in frustration. "But you should have been stopped."

"No! Oh, Mychale, you don't understand. You don't know the whole truth."

He searched her eyes. "Well then, tell me."

She turned from him and led the way to the couch. "Let me catch my breath and I'll tell you everything."

"All right," he said, sitting down beside her. "I'm listening."

She nodded, looking at his face as though she would never get her fill of it. "First tell me what they are saying. What do you think the truth is?"

He shrugged. "Your sister died in childbirth. Whether from grief or jealousy, whatever, you stole her baby— the baby that also belongs to my brother Dane—and went into hiding."

She closed her eyes and tried hard to hold back the tears. "From jealousy?" she whispered. "Is that what my uncle is saying?"

He took her shoulders again. "Tell me your side of this, Abby. Tell me quickly."

She drew air deep into her lungs, lifted her chin and

began. "Julienne did die in childbirth. She ran away when my uncle realized she was pregnant. It took me weeks to find her, and when I did, it was too late. She was in a dirty rat-hole of an apartment in Tapion City with only an ill-trained midwife to help her. Brianna was fine but Julienne was bleeding and the midwife didn't know how to stop it. I called an ambulance and they raced her to the hospital but she had lost too much blood."

He groaned, knowing how hard that must have been. "I wish I'd been there to help you."

She smiled through her tears. "So do I. But there was no one. My uncle was furious. As far as he was concerned, he'd lost an asset and gained another liability. We brought the baby home and I arranged for what she needed. My uncle hardly seemed to care if Brianna lived or died. I thought from the first that I would be Brianna's mother. I'd promised Julienne and anyway, there was no one else. I welcomed the responsibility. Very soon, I was so attached to her, I might as well be her biological mother. She is mine and I am hers."

He nodded. He'd seen that with his own eyes.

"And then, suddenly, my uncle changed. I could tell he had a new scheme. I just didn't know what it was." She hesitated. "I think I explained to you how he took us in from the start thinking we would be useful to him and his ambitions. He tried to get us matches with the nobility, and when he failed at that, he began trying to marry us off to lesser and older noblemen. We resisted. He became more and more angry with us. And at the same time, his contacts in the top levels of royalty and government were slipping away. When your father, King Nevander, died, he lost his most important champion and he was very much afraid of losing all his standing and power. He didn't trust you of the younger generation. He knew you didn't like him much. He'd been casting about for a long time, trying to think of a way to consolidate his position. And then, he decided to use Brianna."

"Go on."

"Everyone knew about the tabloid preoccupation with Dane and his supposedly missing baby. So my uncle thought, why couldn't Brianna be that child? His coming forward with the much-sought-after baby—a baby he is biologically connected to—would surely put him in a position to hang on to power for that much longer."

Mychale was shaking his head in disbelief. "Are you saying she's not Dane's?"

"Of course she's not. I saw the man Julienne had the affair with. I only saw him once, but I can guarantee it wasn't your brother. He was an actor from the school where she was taking classes. She was crazy about him and only found out he was already married when she told him she was pregnant."

"That doesn't make it impossible that she might have been with Dane as well."

"No. But the fact that our uncle sent us both off to Geneva to stay with a colleague of his while Dane was in his care does. We never saw him. Uncle got us out of the way. It was the end of the war and everything seemed to be falling apart. We spent that entire month out of the country."

"But the DNA…"

"Oh, Mychale, he faked it. He's the doctor, he can set up false records and everyone believes them." She clutched his arm. "Have an independent test done. You'll see."

He was frowning down at her. He believed her, but he wasn't sure he had fully taken in all the facts and their ramifications as yet. "Abby, if all this is true, why didn't you tell me from the first?"

She threw out her hands, palms up. "Would you have believed me? I couldn't fight against my uncle and all his lies. I'm nobody. No one would have believed me." She shook her head. "They would think I was just jealous of my sister."

He winced. "Abby, I'm sorry. I should have known better."

She searched his eyes. "Do you believe me?"

"Abby, I told you once you were good as gold. And I still believe it."

Closing her eyes, she sighed as she melted into his arms. "Oh, Mychale, it's such a relief to have the running over with. Please hold me. Hold me tight."

He held her tight, and he kissed her hard, and she responded like a flower opening on a sunny day. All his love poured into her. He'd never known a woman like this. He had to have her and keep her forever safe. His hands slid down her side, taking in the womanly shapes he was sure to make his own and he pulled her up tightly against his own body. He knew she could feel how much he wanted her. It was important to him that she know. He was taking possession, body and soul. From now on, they had to be together.

"Oh God, I've missed you so much," he murmured close to her ear. "Abby, don't ever run away from me again."

She laughed softly. "Never," she promised. "And you promise me that you'll make sure Brianna is taken care of while I'm in prison."

"Prison!" He looked fierce. "Over my dead body."

"But I'll have to go at first, at least until there is a trial or…"

"There is not going to be any trial." The thought of her in that situation brought out his autocratic side right away and he spoke with confidence. That just wasn't going to happen. He wasn't going to let it happen. "You didn't do anything wrong. We'll make sure everyone knows it." His face changed. "But where is Brianna?"

"Downstairs." She jumped up. "Old Mrs. Grunmar must be wondering what's become of me. I usually put away the groceries and then go down and collect the baby."

"Let's go," he said. "I want to see her."

Mrs. Grunmar was in the hall, getting ready to come up and see what was keeping Abby. Brianna was in her arms. She turned her little head, caught sight of the prince and gurgled happily, throwing out both arms toward him.

"You see?" he said, taking her from the older woman. "Abby, did you see that?"

"Involuntary reflex," Abby teased gently. "Don't get cocky."

Holding the baby was almost as delicious as holding Abby—only in a very different way. What was that odd feeling he had as he walked out to his car with the two of them? Joy? Happiness? Wonder at how great life could be? All those things and more. And he didn't let himself think about the bad times to come. He had a focus now. He was going marry Abby. Even if he had to arrange a ceremony in the prison. But hopefully, it wouldn't come to that. It was going to take all his strength and skill, but he was going to do everything in his power to keep Abby free. And her little baby, too.

Abby jumped up from her chair by the window, throwing down her book and making a quick, rather awkward curtsy.

"Your highness," she said, coloring as Crown Prince Dane entered her room. "Welcome. Please come in."

She flashed a questioning look at Mychale who was behind him. She only wished he had warned her the Crown Prince was finally coming to see the baby.

She and Brianna had been staying in this room in a remote part of the palace for over a week now while DNA tests were being analyzed. It was a form of house arrest and she knew how lucky she was to be here rather than in a jail cell. But she'd been living on edge, waiting and wondering what the tests would reveal. There was always the chance that her uncle had influence that could somehow skew the results. If evidence revealed that Brianna actually did have royal family DNA, she knew she was in big trouble. Not only would she lose the baby, but she would lose her freedom and any hope for a future.

Mychale seemed to believe her, but he was reserved when he came for his daily visits. He only opened up with joy when Brianna was awake and responding to him as she always did. She was beginning to think he was growing to love Brianna as much as she did. He'd certainly gone to bat for her with Dane, insisting she be given a room here in the palace, insisting she be treated as a sort of guest rather than a criminal.

Of the rest of the family, only Carla had come by. She'd been even more reserved than Mychale, but after she'd visited once, she came again and again. Abby had a feeling they could become good friends if all worked out as it should.

But would it? Now here was Dane, looking serious, with Mychale behind him, looking noncommittal. Had the results come in?

"May I see the child?" Dane asked.

"Of course."

She turned and lifted Brianna from the crib where she was sleeping, her heart beating a ragged rhythm in her chest. Why would he want to see the baby, unless there had been some indication he was the father? If that was the case, she was sunk.

"She's beautiful," he murmured, stroking her little cheek but making no attempt to take her himself. "I'm almost sorry she's not mine."

"Oh!" Abby looked quickly from Dane to Mychale and back again. "The DNA…?"

"Came back negative," Dane said. "You were telling the truth. I only wish you'd told it from the beginning so we wouldn't all have had to go through this."

Relief made her feel faint for a moment. Mychale stepped forward and took Brianna from her.

"She didn't feel she had any choice, you know," he began, defending Abby to his brother.

"I know, I know," Dane said, waving the explanation away impatiently. "And I am glad you made sure we knew the truth; even if the clarification was a bit tardy." He shrugged. "You're free to go. Your uncle has fled the country. But we'll find him."

With a short, stiff bow, he turned and left the room. Abby looked up at Mychale. He was smiling, holding a very sleepy Brianna to his chest. Abby didn't say a word but her eyes filled with tears which began to stream down her cheeks.

"Hold on," Mychale said, looking alarmed. "Let me put Brianna down."

That only took him a moment, and then his arms were around Abby and he was holding her close, kissing the top of her head as she sobbed against his chest. "Hey, it's all over," he murmured, kissing her wet face as she looked up. "Everything's going to be okay."

"Oh, Mychale, thank you so much. I can't believe the danger is gone. Will I be allowed to keep Brianna as my own?"

He nodded, smiling down at her. "Of course. It's all been settled." His expression shifted. "I'm sorry I haven't been acting as natural as I would have liked with you. I believed you, Abby. But I felt I had to support my family until your story was verified. I hated acting cool to you. I hope you can forgive me."

"Forgive you?" She laughed through her tears. "Only if you can forgive me for lying to you at the château."

"It's a deal." He kissed her warm mouth. "And here's another. Abby Donair, mother of Brianna, will you marry me?"

Abby's eyes widened with shock.

"How can I marry you? You need to marry someone who will help the royal family strengthen its foundations and build the country and…"

"No, Abby." His hands framed her face. "I need to marry someone I love, someone I can live with for the rest of my life. And you are that person." He dropped a kiss on her full lips. "So how about it? Yes or no?"

Abby closed her eyes and breathed in the air around her. She felt as though she were in a magic place, living a magic life. And when she opened her eyes, her prince was still there.

"Yes," she told him, her eyes full of love for him. "Oh, yes!"

EPILOGUE

THERE were plans to be made, loose ends to tie up, papers to be signed. Always more papers to be signed.

"Tell me, what about Gregor?" Abby asked at one point, as they were setting out a schedule for their return to the lake country a month into the future. "You said Dane was to interview him to take over my uncle's job, at least for now."

Mychale nodded. "Dane was pleased with him. He's the logical replacement, as he knows more about the royal family's health than anyone else and only needs to meet a few bureaucratic requirements to fully qualify."

"Good."

Mychale shook his head. "Don't celebrate too soon. Carla vetoed the whole thing. She wouldn't hear of it."

That was a surprise. "What? I can't believe that. They were friends in the old days."

He shrugged, frowning. "I'll talk to her and see if I can figure out what the problem is. We'll get this fixed." These days it seemed as though anything could be fixed. Looking down at her, he smiled. Every time he looked at her it happened. Smiles just came natu-rally around her. "In the meantime, we have a wedding to plan."

He was insisting on a public wedding at the main cathedral, where royal weddings had always been held.

"I'm not going to be quiet about loving Abby," he told Dane. "I'm not like Nico. He and Marisa married in secret, but that was his way. He likes to manipulate from behind the scenes. I've always been featured in the news. It would seem as though I weren't totally committed to Abby and Brianna if I didn't make a public spectacle of my wedding. Don't you see that?"

"You can't have a full state wedding until our family is officially installed once again," his brother had answered. "That will have to wait until I've taken the crown."

Mychale groaned. "I understand that. We don't want a major event here. Something simple. Just a normal, family wedding."

"A normal family wedding that the whole country is in on," Dane grumbled.

"Well, yes. But nothing too extreme."

Dane looked pained. "I take it we can avoid the gold-encrusted carriages and full regimental ten-gun salutes?"

"Sure." Mychale frowned doubtfully. "If we must."

In the end, Dane relented. The cathedral was prepared and the city was tastefully decorated for the wedding. The idea was to keep everything open but low-key. The trouble was, the people of Carnethia had other ideas. After all the years of war and uncertainty, they were thrilled to have a royal wedding to celebrate. As soon as the news was out, every house, every shop, every park was festooned with streamers and banners proclaiming joy and best wishes for the happy couple.

At the same time, the tabloids were going crazy trying to figure out whose baby was whose and what had happened to Dr. Zavier and just exactly what was going on in that thing they considered the royal shell game. As usual, they were getting everything wrong. And Mychale didn't care.

"I wash my hands of it all. If everything they said about us was half-true, we would be the most exciting family on the planet. I'm all for ignoring them. Let them print what they want. I'm going to live my life the way I want to live it and I'm not going to be second-guessing everything through their lens."

But all the controversy made Abby uneasy. Held safe in the circle of Mychale's arms, she looked up and searched his eyes.

"Are you sure we should marry? Are you really, really sure?"

He smiled down at her. "I've never been more sure of anything in my life." He dropped a kiss on her soft lips. "How about you? Are you sure?"

She frowned tentatively. "I think so."

He shook his head, troubled by her doubts. "Why do you hesitate?"

"I don't know. It seems like a big step for you. A step away from the path you were meant to take. If you have any qualms…"

Mychale grunted without answering, pulling away and taking a stack of papers from his briefcase. "Here," he said. "So much for your talk of 'qualms.'"

She stared at the papers and absently took the pen he handed her. "What are these for?"

"Adoption papers for Brianna."

She scanned them quickly, noting the places marked for two signatures. "For both of us?" Looking up at him, she glowed.

He smiled into her eyes. "Of course."

"Then we will truly, truly be her parents?"

"Yes."

She sighed. "Oh, Mychale, I *will* marry you."

He laughed softly as he pulled her back into his arms. "Are you telling me that you were only trembling on the brink until this adoption pushed you over?"

But there were no words spoken because her kiss was all the answer he needed.

The day of the wedding dawned bright and clear. The whole city was electric with anticipation. Abby moved in a dream, letting the chattering entourage dress her in lace and pearls while her full attention was captured by tending to Brianna. Carla and Nadia rode with her in the carriage. They kept up a teasing exchange, but she hardly heard them. The streets were thronged with happy crowds. But it all seemed a blur to her, until she started down the aisle and saw Mychale waiting for her at the end of the velvet carpet.

He looked as handsome as any man she'd ever seen in his full dress uniform, a sword at his side. She almost swooned at the sight of him, but his welcoming smile kept her safe and she walked toward it slowly, savoring every step. The priest was talking about how their union would form one of the foundations of this renewed country. That made her proud. But even more important to her, she was marrying the man she loved, the man who loved her child.

She spoke her vows out loud and clear, and when it was over, she turned to Mychale with joy. This was it. And now, to live happily ever after.

* * * * *

Don't miss the exciting conclusion of this miniseries next month with
FOUND: HIS ROYAL BABY!

Turn the page for a sneak preview of
AFTERSHOCK, *a new anthology*
featuring New York Times *bestselling author*
Sharon Sala.

Available October 2008.

n o c t u r n e ™

Dramatic and sensual tales of paranormal romance.

Chapter 1

October
New York City

Nicole Masters was sitting cross-legged on her sofa while a cold autumn rain peppered the windows of her fourth-floor apartment. She was poking at the ice cream in her bowl and trying not to be in a mood.

Six weeks ago, a simple trip to her neighborhood pharmacy had turned into a nightmare. She'd walked into the middle of a robbery. She never even saw the man who shot her in the head and left her for dead. She'd survived, but some of her senses had not. She was dealing with short-term memory loss and a tendency to stagger. Even though she'd been told the problems were most likely temporary, she waged a daily battle with depression.

Her parents had been killed in a car wreck when she was twenty-one. And except for a few friends—and most recently her boyfriend, Dominic Tucci, who lived in the apartment right above hers, she was alone. Her doctor kept reminding her that she should be grateful to be alive, and on one level she knew he was right. But he wasn't living in her shoes.

If she'd been anywhere else but at that pharmacy when the robbery happened, she wouldn't have died twice on the way to the hospital. Instead of being grateful that she'd survived, she couldn't stop thinking of what she'd lost.

But that wasn't the end of her troubles. On top of everything else, something strange was happening inside her head. She'd begun to hear odd things: sounds, not voices—at least, she didn't think it was voices. It was more like the distant noise of rapids—a rush of wind and water inside her head that, when it came, blocked out everything around her. It didn't happen often, but when it did, it was frightening, and it was driving her crazy.

The blank moments, which is what she called them, even had a rhythm. First there came that sound, then a cold sweat, then panic with no reason. Part of her feared it was the beginning of an emotional breakdown. And part of her feared it wasn't—that it was going to turn out to be a permanent souvenir of her resurrection.

Frustrated with herself and the situation as it stood, she upped the sound on the TV remote. But instead of *Wheel of Fortune,* an announcer broke in with a special bulletin.

"This just in. Police are on the scene of a kidnapping that occurred only hours ago at The Dakota. Molly Dane, the six-year-old daughter of one of Hollywood's blockbuster stars, Lyla Dane, was taken by force from the family apartment. At this time they have yet to receive a ransom demand.

The housekeeper was seriously injured during the abduction, and is, at the present time, in surgery. Police are hoping to be able to talk to her once she regains consciousness. In the meantime, we are going now to a press conference with Lyla Dane."

Horrified, Nicole stilled as the cameras went live to where the actress was speaking before a bank of microphones. The shock and terror in Lyla Dane's voice were physically painful to watch. But even though Nicole kept upping the volume, the sound continued to fade.

Just when she was beginning to think something was wrong with her set, the broadcast suddenly switched from the Dane press conference to what appeared to be footage of the kidnapping, beginning with footage from inside the apartment.

When the front door suddenly flew back against the wall and four men rushed in, Nicole gasped. Horrified, she quickly realized that this must have been caught on a security camera inside the Dane apartment.

As Nicole continued to watch, a small Asian woman, who she guessed was the maid, rushed forward in an effort to keep them out. When one of the men hit her in the face with his gun, Nicole moaned. The violence was too reminiscent of what she'd lived through. Sick to her stomach, she fisted her hands against her belly, wishing it was over, but unable to tear her gaze away.

When the maid dropped to the carpet, the same man followed with a vicious kick to the little woman's midsection that lifted her off the floor.

"Oh, my God," Nicole said. When blood began to pool beneath the maid's head, she started to cry.

As the tape played on, the four men split up in different directions. The camera caught one running down a long marble hallway, then disappearing into a room. Moments later he reappeared, carrying a little girl, who Nicole assumed was Molly Dane. The child was wearing a pair of red pants and a white turtleneck sweater, and her hair was partially blocking her abductor's face as he carried her down the hall. She was kicking and screaming in his arms, and when he slapped her, it elicited an agonized scream that brought the other three running. Nicole watched in horror as one of them ran up and put his hand over Molly's face. Seconds later, she went limp.

One moment they were in the foyer, then they were gone.

Nicole jumped to her feet, then staggered drunkenly. The bowl of ice cream she'd absentmindedly placed in her lap shattered at her feet, splattering glass and melting ice cream everywhere.

The picture on the screen abruptly switched from the kidnapping to what Nicole assumed was a rerun of Lyla Dane's plea for her daughter's safe return, but she was numb.

Before she could think what to do next, the doorbell rang. Startled by the unexpected sound, she shakily swiped at the tears and took a step forward. She didn't feel the glass shards piercing her feet until she took the second step. At that point, sharp pains shot through her foot. She gasped, then looked down in confusion. Her legs looked as if she'd been running through mud, and she was standing in broken glass and ice cream, while a thin ribbon of blood seeped out from beneath her toes.

"Oh, no," Nicole mumbled, then stifled a second moan of pain.

The doorbell rang again. She shivered, then clutched her head in confusion.

"Just a minute!" she yelled, then tried to sidestep the rest of the debris as she hobbled to the door.

When she looked through the peephole in the door, she didn't know whether to be relieved or regretful.

It was Dominic, and as usual, she was a mess.

Nicole smiled a little self-consciously as she opened the door to let him in. "I just don't know what's happening to me. I think I'm losing my mind."

"Hey, don't talk about my woman like that."

Nicole rode the surge of delight his words brought. "So I'm still your woman?"

Dominic lowered his head.

Their lips met.

The kiss proceeded.

Slowly.

Thoroughly.

* * * * *

Be sure to look for the **AFTERSHOCK** *anthology next month, as well as other exciting paranormal stories from Silhouette Nocturne.*
Available in October wherever books are sold.

nocturne™

NEW YORK TIMES BESTSELLING AUTHOR

SHARON SALA

JANIS REAMES HUDSON
DEBRA COWAN

AFTERSHOCK

Three women are brought to the brink of death...
only to discover the aftershock of their trauma has
left them with unexpected and unwelcome gifts of
paranormal powers. Now each woman must learn to
accept her newfound abilities while fighting for life,
love and second chances....

Available October wherever books are sold.

www.eHarlequin.com
www.paranormalromanceblog.wordpress.com

SN61796

SPECIAL EDITION™

BRAVO FAMILY TIES

Tanner Bravo and Crystal Cerise had it bad
for each other, though they couldn't be more
different. Tanner was the type to settle down;
free-spirited Crystal wouldn't hear of it.
Now that Crystal was pregnant, would
Tanner have his way after all?

Look for

HAVING
TANNER BRAVO'S
BABY

by *USA TODAY* bestselling author
CHRISTINE RIMMER

Available in October wherever books are sold.

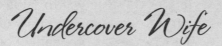

Silhouette®
Romantic
SUSPENSE

**Sparked by Danger,
Fueled by Passion.**

USA TODAY bestselling author

Merline Lovelace

Undercover Wife

Secret agent Mike Callahan, code name Hawkeye,
objects when he's paired with sophisticated
Gillian Ridgeway on a dangerous spy mission
to Hong Kong. Gillian has secretly been in love
with him for years, but Hawk is an overprotective
man with a wounded past that threatens to
resurface. Now the two must put their lives—
and hearts—at risk for each other.

Available October wherever books are sold.

REQUEST YOUR FREE BOOKS!
2 FREE NOVELS PLUS 2
FREE GIFTS!

HARLEQUIN ROMANCE®

From the Heart, For the Heart

YES! Please send me 2 FREE Harlequin Romance® novels and my 2 FREE gifts (gifts are worth about $10). After receiving them, if I don't wish to receive any more books, I can return the shipping statement marked "cancel." If I don't cancel, I will receive 4 brand-new novels every month and be billed just $3.32 per book in the U.S. or $3.80 per book in Canada, plus 25¢ shipping and handling per book and applicable taxes, if any*. That's a savings of over 15% off the cover price! I understand that accepting the 2 free books and gifts places me under no obligation to buy anything. I can always return a shipment and cancel at any time. Even if I never buy another book, the two free books and gifts are mine to keep forever.

114 HDN ERQW   314 HDN ERQ9

Name	(PLEASE PRINT)	
Address		Apt. #
City	State/Prov.	Zip/Postal Code

Signature (if under 18, a parent or guardian must sign)

Mail to the **Harlequin Reader Service:**
IN U.S.A.: P.O. Box 1867, Buffalo, NY 14240-1867
IN CANADA: P.O. Box 609, Fort Erie, Ontario L2A 5X3

Not valid to current subscribers of Harlequin Romance books.

Want to try two free books from another line?
Call 1-800-873-8635 or visit www.morefreebooks.com.

* Terms and prices subject to change without notice. N.Y. residents add applicable sales tax. Canadian residents will be charged applicable provincial taxes and GST. Offer not valid in Quebec. This offer is limited to one order per household. All orders subject to approval. Credit or debit balances in a customer's account(s) may be offset by any other outstanding balance owed by or to the customer. Please allow 4 to 6 weeks for delivery. Offer available while quantities last.

Your Privacy: Harlequin Books is committed to protecting your privacy. Our Privacy Policy is available online at www.eHarlequin.com or upon request from the Reader Service. From time to time we make our lists of customers available to reputable third parties who may have a product or service of interest to you. If you would prefer we not share your name and address, please check here. ☐

HR08R

Harlequin® Historical
Historical Romantic Adventure!

HALLOWE'EN
HUSBANDS

With three fantastic stories by

Lisa Plumley
Denise Lynn
Christine Merrill

Don't miss these unforgettable
stories about three women who
experience the mysterious
happenings of Allhallows Eve
and come to discover that finding
true love on this eerie day is not
so scary after all.

Look for
HALLOWE'EN HUSBANDS

Available October
wherever books are sold.

HARLEQUIN Romance.

Coming Next Month

Handsome sheep barons, maverick tycoons and dashing princes— you can find them all in Harlequin Romance®!

#4051 BRIDE AT BRIAR'S RIDGE Margaret Way

In the second of the *Barons of the Outback* duet, Daniela Adami comes to Wangaree Valley to escape her life in London. Her heart is guarded, but when handsome sheep baron Linc Mastermann strides into her world, he turns it upside down....

#4052 FOUND: HIS ROYAL BABY Raye Morgan

Crown Prince Dane—the third of the *Royals of Montenevada*—has heard rumors of a secret royal baby. With the kingdom in uproar, his only choice is to confront Alexandra Acredonna—the woman who still haunts his dreams....

#4053 THE MILLIONAIRE'S NANNY ARRANGEMENT Linda Goodnight
Baby on Board

The only thing businessman Ryan Storm can't give his six-year-old daughter is a mom—but he can hire the next best thing.... Pregnant and widowed, Kelsey Mason isn't Ryan's idea of the perfect nanny—but little Mariah bonds with her straight away, and soon he starts to fall under her spell....

#4054 LAST-MINUTE PROPOSAL Jessica Hart

Cake-baker Tilly is taking part in a charity job-swap, but when she's paired with ex-military chief executive Campbell Sanderson, Campbell is all hard angles to Tilly's cozy curves. But something about her always makes him smile. And then they share a showstopping kiss....

#4055 HIRED: THE BOSS'S BRIDE Ally Blake
9 to 5

Mitch Hanover needed a miracle—someone to bring life to his business— and when Veronica Bing roared up in her pink Corvette and told him she was the girl for the job, he couldn't help but agree! But even though attraction zinged between them, Mitch had sworn never to love again....

#4056 THE SINGLE MOM AND THE TYCOON Caroline Anderson

Handsome millionaire David Cauldwell is blown away by sexy single mom Molly Blythe. He can see she and her young son need his love as much as he yearns for theirs—but falling in love means taking risks: David must face the secret that changed his life....

HRCNM0908